D0240250

the book of shadows

Also by Namita Gokhale

PARO: DREAMS OF PASSION

GODS, GRAVES AND GRANDMOTHER

A HIMALAYAN LOVE STORY

MOUNTAIN ECHOES

the book of shadows

namita gokhale

Little, Brown and Company

A *Little, Brown* Book

First published in Great Britain in 2000
by Little, Brown and Company
First published in India in 1999 by Penguin Books India

A CIP catalogue record for this book
is available from the British Library.

ISBN 0 316 85155 8

Typeset in Garamond by M Rules
Printed and bound in Great Britain by Clays Ltd, St Ives plc

Little, Brown and Company (UK)
Brettenham House
Lancaster Place
London WC2E 7EN

Author's Note

I too have lived in the house I have written about. This is a novel which has its core in truth. It has been written, or it has written itself, under circumstances which would appear strange to most people. It has been a vehicle to resolve my personal pain, but there is more to it than that. My gratitude to R.S. (both of them) I.R.C. and A.C.

I.i

My intention is to tell of bodies changed to different forms.

Ovid, *Metamorphoses*

The tortured oaks lean against each other, their groping limbs invading the territories of other trees. They draw strange screeching sounds as bark brushes sap, and the shadows of the forest start speaking in the dark. The pines sigh in the evenings as though with one voice. These are my only companions. This house belongs to me, as I belong to this house. I live here alone in the hills, watching the day turn to dusk, awaiting the dawn. This house, which knew me as a child, has taken me in again. It will never reject those who love it. We have closed ranks together, me and the house. We have become as one spirit, it is us against the world. All day I sit and stare at the blinding shadows of the snows. I sit here by the window and shelter in the certainty of these presences, so different from the bewildering world below. I belong to this house, as this house belongs to me.

Who am I? This essentially philosophical question has suddenly assumed a tangible immediacy. We define ourselves by the people that we know, by the face we see in the mirror. In my case all the parameters have changed. I can feel the doors to self-knowledge banging shut upon me. Even the face I meet in the mirror is no longer mine. Although it is to an extent familiar it is mostly strange. In those long-ago days when I taught English literature at

Jesus and Mary College, when I was myself an earnest overgrown student masquerading as an academic, I tried to explain the concept of alienation to my students. Rich young girls from Punjabi Bagh, without a care in the world beyond their next shampoo, creased their perfectly threaded eyebrows in puzzled if polite concentration and accosted the problem.

'Alienation is a device to make the unfamiliar familiar,' I said, addressing a sea of guileless faces, 'or to render the familiar unfamiliar.' I was merely being clever, I was gassing a bit, I knew I was safe in that my audience wasn't even listening to me, but I was wrong. In every classroom in the world there is one disconcerting student with the gift of being right at the wrong time. Zenobia Desai was an oversized girl with a moustache and gentle eyes. She raised her hand, and when I ignored her she stood up and spoke her piece. 'Excuse me, Ma'am,' she said, 'excuse me, I was discussing this with my boyfriend, and we agreed that the stamp of alienation is the loss of identity.'

There was a convulsion of smirks and surprised looks at her intervention. 'You mean you actually have a boyfriend, Zenobia?!' a pert young thing exclaimed mockingly. 'Who's your boyfriend, Frankenstein?!!' That was of course a lifetime ago, just last term in linear time, but linear time has retreated from my life suspended by an oblong noose of rope hanging from a ceiling fan, the sound of a cicada chirruping in the woodwork breaking the heavy silence with its insistent trills as the grotesque figure of my fiancé Anand swung gently in the centre of the empty room.

Anand's tongue, the tongue I had known from his kisses, hung from the corner of his mouth like some comic caricature. It leered at me, it jeered at my surprise, it was purple and pink and the spit had not yet dried on it. Who was this swaying on a rope before me? This was not my gentle lover, the stroker of my brow. It was an unbearable excess of all that was possible and bearable. I could not catch Anand's eye, he was staring with something resembling surprise not at me but at the upturned chair beneath him. The curtain stirred and through the still silence of the hot June night I could hear the distant roar of departing traffic echoing like an ocean in my head.

There was defeat here, and a loss of dignity. This travesty of not-life was not how death was to be faced: of this I was sure.

There was a long suicide note, written in Anand's sloping italic hand, which went something like this. 'Goodbye, cruel world! I bid thee farewell! You have tried me sorely, you have abused my trust! My tryst with time is over! Tell the faithless one, the Delilah, that her betrayal will cost her dear' and so on.

Well, I had betrayed him, I had 'yielded to passion', as he put it, to the not so gentle persuasions of my best friend's husband. Unreality gets compounded by confusion. My best friend's husband had slithered off somewhere, but my fiancé's sister, as unstable a specimen as her sibling, had thrown a bottle of acid into my face the day after the inquest.

I had encountered her as I was re-contouring the shadow on my eyes in the misty mirror in the bogs next to the cafeteria. There's a separate dressing room for staff and faculty upstairs, but I didn't want to face the other teachers: this was my first day in college after Anand's death.

And then it happened. As my vision blurred, as my consciousness dissolved in a river of pain I could hear the tinkle of her bangles, glass against gold, and the swish of her starched cotton sari as she walked out, leaving me alone in the toilet block. I tried to reach for the water tap, I realised it was the thing to do, but even as I dragged myself across the smooth mosaic floor I knew that although the first monsoon clouds had gathered themselves around Delhi the taps would inevitably be dry. The pain, the unbearable pain, and then a giggling group of freshers stunned into silence and Sister Melba escorting me to the infirmary upstairs.

Anand's sister had taught Chemistry at the same college where I tried to perpetuate the study of English Literature. Insanity obviously ran in their family, as also the tendency to take recourse to extreme action upon the slightest provocation. Just my luck.

Reality pressed upon me with the weight of the unshed August clouds, it confronted me in the eyes of strangers, it afforded me no relief in this crowded relentless city I had once called my home.

I have come to the hills to heal, to hide, to forget. To forgive, to be forgiven. My friends all resisted my decision, my sister tried to insist she accompany me here, but I knew that I needed silence and solitude and soliloquy to come to terms with what had happened. My name was in every newspaper. The press took a morbid interest in all that had happened in the course of that summer madness; pictures of my face as it had been stared back at me from everywhere. The acid had worked on the bone cartilage, and the surgeon had been cautious in his restorations. I have not looked at a mirror for months now, and my face, that familiar index of my being, has dissolved into absurdity and abstraction.

Even my fingers do not recognise the changed contours of my cheeks, of the broken flesh. The avengers of my vanity have broken me, humbled me with these small depredations of skin and bone and tissue, leaving me less than I was.

Where am I? My mother was from these mountains, and I had known this house as a child, spent many happy summers here. It belongs to my mother's brother, my mamaji. He lives in Bangalore now (my parents are both dead) and since he has no children the house will one day probably belong to us, to my sister and to me.

I already belong to this house. It has taken me in, enveloped my hurt. It soothes my hatred, hushes my sorrow. It had been hostile at first, it was angry that we had forgotten the sanctuary of its love. This old and gentle house, built by a missionary a hundred years ago, was the repository of my youth, the custodian of my dreams. I had been happy here as a child, and I am determined to be that again, to forget Anand's indulgent and wanton act of self-destruction, ignore his stupidity, and restore my life to its own course once again. You see, I have all the right intentions.

After I was discharged from the hospital, Delhi appeared a wilderness of heartbreak and pain. I travelled up to the hills alone, in a rickety clattering deathtrap of a taxi. I covered up my face with a long muslin chunni, bedouin style, and observed the familiar changes of landscape on the journey up. As we approached Ranikhet I caught my breath in wonder. In Delhi I always forget how beautiful our hills are. The Kathgodam road witnesses some incredible changes of scenery, and the last bit before Ranikhet, with its miles and miles of abandoned terraced fields, is almost frightening in its desolation. We took the other road, from Ramnagar. Even though it was late June and the Himalayas were covered in a haze of dust and heat, we had snatches and visitations of their presences all the way through.

The house is set some distance from the main road. There is a deep dip into a small ravine, where a stream flows rapidly through the hillside until it reaches the turn, as though it were running away from somebody, escaping pursuit. The pine and deodar forests suddenly close in, and an outsider might find something menacing about the air. The thick undergrowth and overhanging vines add to the effect. The taxi driver, a tired old Sikh with an air of melancholy resignation, voiced his doubts about our destination. 'This place looks absolutely junglee,' he said, a note of concern in his voice. 'There must be wild animals around here, not to speak of thieves and robbers. Do you really want to go on? We could find a nice hotel in Ranikhet.'

I urged him on, lying about the distance to the house. The exhausted taxi wheezed and coughed towards the hilltop, through the winding *kuchha* road with its stones and boulders and exposed tree roots. The splats of cow dung that marked our path seemed almost reassuring, indicating the presence of domestic animals. Two giggling *ghasyarans*, local girls in bright blue petticoats, with sickles in their hands and bundles of fodder balanced on their pretty heads, met us as we passed. They stared after us curiously. I'm sure they hadn't seen a car in these parts for years.

As we neared the house a familiar sense of elation overtook me. The very air here is different, it is thinner and purer than city air, its pine-scented effervescence made me feel heady and expectant. The taxi driver was getting more and more alarmed. 'Maybe we should turn back now,' he said timidly. 'I don't think this road leads anywhere.'

I knew better. At the next turn of the road we would meet the gates of the house, and the old outhouse where I had played as a child. The hillside was covered with patches of wild narcissus. A Himalayan bird of paradise made a low swoop across the road, as though in welcome. A pair of marmots, what our hill people call 'chitrail', swerved before us, panicking at the intrusion of the car. A hoopoe balanced on a clump of bamboo and piped out a tune.

The thickets of bamboo on either side of the road arched and met high in the air. The haze cleared up for a brief second, and the numinous outline of Nanda Devi, its summer snows gleaming in the afternoon sun, greeted us. Even the driver was disarmed, and a tentative smile played upon his bearded face.

There is a last twist and curve to the road, and then we came to the house. There it stood, in all its loveliness. A gracious veranda encircled its contours. The white blooms of climbing roses clung to the frontage. The windows of the upstairs bedrooms gazed out at the sweep of the Himalayan ranges, now obscured from view. Broken stone steps led down from the garden to the tennis court below, or to what had once been the tennis court, but was now but an overgrowth of bramble and nettle. The garden was covered with dandelion and forget-me-not, although some clumps of lupin and larkspur struggled against the chaos of weed. The two hydrangea bushes were where they had always been; they had grown to monstrous proportions, the blue flowers streaked and spotted with purple.

The driver extracted the two suitcases from the boot of the car and decided to abandon me. The taxi disappeared in a bustle of groaning and hooting. The smell of diesel hung in the air, offending my nostrils. The muslin chunni and the bedouin mask had fallen from my face. There was no one here I needed to hide from.

I was overtaken by what, for want of a better word, I can only describe as a sense of *déjà vu.* I had been here before, to this very spot, not in my anterior history as a child or a young girl, but in this very form and this very time. There was an overlay of perception and memory, a mass of recollection that struggled to be set free.

The front door was locked. I would have to call Lohaniju from the servants' quarters. I had not bothered to inform him of my arrival.

A swarm of yellow butterflies appeared out of nowhere They settled themselves on the roses, on the overgrown hydrangeas, they hovered in midair like a celestial garden. Some impress of memory was set loose from my mind. Images fluttered out of nowhere and sprung to life in full form. A procession of people came out from all directions to meet me. They stood there, in the flesh, no phantoms or fantasies but people like you or me. Some I could see clearly, and others evaded recognition. A woman with a bunch of summer flowers in her hand, a woman of surpassing beauty with a sheath of static surrounding her. Two strange figures, cowering in the sunlight, pale personages of undistinguished demeanour. A local *Pahari* youth, his face hooded in a woollen shawl, a blood red slash across his pale forehead.

In the distance I could hear the yowling of dogs, their sad insistent barking which dissolved into a sort of collective sigh. The putrid stench of decomposition arose from somewhere around me, followed by the smell of narcissus. The smell was so powerful that it unlocked some secret cache of memory, some hidden intimation of what had been. Snatches of sound filled the air, melody not lyric. These were not strangers around me, they were familiar cohabitants of the same space. It was as though we had escaped the confines of our life-scripts, stumbled upon some interstice of experience, some simultaneity of narrative. But who was the narrator?

Just then Lohaniju came loping out of the house. His long legs and lanky, almost adolescent gait filled me with a rush of relief Lohaniju was there, I was home again.

*

I am on medication: antibiotics and anxiolytics. I have Lohaniju to look after me, our old servant Lohaniju, in his eighties now, still tall and strong and garrulous in the extreme. Lohaniju loves the house, he has lived here all his life. He has never been to Nain Tal, never been to Almora. The furthest he has ever ventured from the house is to Ranikhet market, where he goes once a week for the shopping and to pick up the mail.

Lohaniju loves me almost as much as he loves the house, and after my return here he has started off once again upon his interminable stories. He has forgotten how old I am, how old he is. It is as though I am a child again, sitting huddled by the fireplace, where the glow of the embers lights up Lohaniju's unnaturally large ears, making him look like an elf, or like something out of *Star Trek.*

'*O Lucifer, son of the morning, how art thou fallen!*'

Where did that come from? Bits and pieces of all that I have learnt and studied dart about my head like shrapnel. I dodge these high words, this alien language, and seek refuge in Lohaniju's soft and consonated Pahari. The Kumaoni language, Pahari, is accused of being only a dialect, yet it is my mother tongue, its sounds reassure me, silence my puzzlement and pain. Our Lohaniju is a Scheherazade in his own right, his stories end invariably with a glass of warm milk sweetened with jaggery and a cliff-hanger which he promises to resolve the next day.

Lohaniju's stories have beguiled me as long as I can remember. His quicksilver tongue maintains many rhythms and momentums: he is a virtuoso storyteller, and his technique has perfected itself over the years. His enormous jug ears protrude at alarming angles from behind his long mutton-chop side whiskers. Whenever he is about to embark upon one of his stories, his left ear begins to twitch, and Lohaniju tugs at the small gold hoops which glisten on his earlobes. 'That's my twin – my shadow double – telling me not to stray from the truth!' he explains, and for the duration of the story his left index finger remains ringed through the gold hoop to stop his jug ear from twitching

'I'll tell you a story about this old house, Bitiya,' he says, in his story voice, which is deeper and more dramatic than his everyday voice. 'This is the house where I was born, and where my father and grandfather were born before me – you must understand that our family belongs to this house, even if this house does not belong to us. And now, after me, there will be nobody left – no one to look after all the people who live here, to serve my masters.' I usually let that pass, for Lohaniju is growing old, his memory is slipping and his talk is often garbled.

The warm glow from the *sagad*, the native iron stove we have reverted to, and Kishore Kumar in the background. Or the Doors, sometimes, with their songs of alienation.

Anyway, perfect atmospherics and all that, Lohaniju's finger looped securely into his earring, his ear breaking into a little twitch every now and then. 'This house – what should I tell you about this house? What should I not tell you about this house? Perhaps silence is indeed better. That's what the ancient Vedas say. *Maunam Sarvam Sadhanam.* Silence is always the best option. But I've been silent much too long, with no one to talk to. I'm a garrulous old man, and if I can keep you amused with my wagging tongue and my twitching ear, it's not such a bad thing at all!'

By this stage I normally tire of admiring my perfectly painted fingernails. Sensing my impatience, Lohaniju leaps into the story *in media res.* 'There was an English sahib – two of them really, the sahib and his friend. They were bad people, Bitiya – very bad people! They insulted the spirits of these mountains – they were rude and arrogant and very, very foolish. They were disrespectful, they were not afraid where they should have been, but then, ahaha – our mountain people – they are no less, Bitiya! They taught those Englishmen a lesson, right here in their own house. They tore apart the white men's blood and flesh and spirit until their own mothers would not recognise them if they sought shelter there! Our mountain gods disguised themselves as panthers and attacked the white sahibs, right here in this house, one *Amavasya* night. I swear this is true! It is not one of my stories! Look – even my ear is not twitching!' And indeed it is not, it is solemn and still and affirmative of the truth of Lohaniju's ramblings.

There is another of his stories I love listening to – the one about Airee, the folk god of our hills, whose armour and bows and arrows lie scattered in temples across Kumaon: whose palanquin is carried by monstrous ghouls, followed by a procession of dogs. The Lord Airee figures prominently in Lohaniju's repertoire. Moreover, in the course of these Airee tales his left ear maintains a stoic stillness, its lack of motion eloquent testimonial to their veracity.

'There I was, in the middle of the forest, where the wicked wanton *Daayans* had enticed me with their wiles. I clutched my topknot, I clutched at my sacred thread, I prayed to Shivji, to our Bhoothnath ruler of the nether worlds, I prayed to Lord Airee to save me from their vengeful plans. "Come with us, please," the cunning Daayans said to me, in voices as soft as the moonlight, "come with us, we shall take you to the sacred mountain where the eternal serpent guards the celestial gems." Bitiya, greed has been the downfall of greater souls than mine, but eventually my prayers saved me. "I am just a poor and humble brahmin," I told them.

"Why do you waste your time with the likes of me, O noble ladies?" All this while Airee was testing me; I had angered him, you see. His wrestler's biceps were bulging eagerly for a fight, growing more and more restless in the confines of his palanquin, and the dogs that follow him, they were all sighing in the strangest way – *sau, sau, sau* – an unearthly sound. Well, Bitiya, I held on to my topknot and my sacred thread and, clutching at my dhoti, I ran with the strength of desperation, with the strength that comes after all one's strength has seeped out and one has known the true meaning of fear. I ran and I ran and I ran. When at last I returned to this house, I was out of breath for three whole days!'

'I didn't go to Ranikhet for a month, I didn't want to leave the safety of this house, and the fellows at the post office thought that I was dead. Finally they came here with the mail themselves; there was a money order from Bangalore they brought with them. "We thought you were dead, Lohaniju," they said in relief when they saw me. "It's good to know that you are still alive!"

'Well, I'll let you into a secret, Bitiya – something no one else in the world knows. My daughter, perhaps – she's a sly one, she used to follow me about sometimes – nobody else knows how I survived Airee's wrath. He is a wrestler, you see, and he loves to eat, gobble gobble gobble all the time! The way to his heart is through his stomach, it is a route we poor brahmins understand! I used to hear him sometimes – a bad-tempered shout and then the sighing of his dogs, *sau, sau, sau*! But I knew what to do by now! I'd blow on the fire and bring it to life, and make some thick creamy kheer, the milk boiled just right, the rice dissolved until it could melt in the mouth, and enough jaggery to give us ordinary mortals a toothache. Then I'd creep out into the forest, taking three earthen bowls of the rice pudding with me – and I'd lay them out in the path that leads away from the servants' quarters, the path that leads to the stream. It's not difficult to distract Airee, he has to be propitiated in his own way. Remember, Bitiya, the spirit world is best handled obliquely – rush in headlong and you're finished! It's a question of mutual respect and tolerance, like everything else in this world.'

Lohaniju's ears gleam in the firelight, and a glass of warm milk materialises from somewhere behind him as he concludes his story. Lohaniju has spent his life bending the barriers of truth, and I have always found his fictions irresistible, I have never doubted any word he has ever spoken. Like this house he has taken me in to hush my sorrow. He was born here, in this house, and his father had worked here before him, as the estate-manager for the white men whom Lohaniju holds in such a mixture of reverence and contempt.

'Oh, the stories I can tell you about this house, Bitiya, they would make your hair stand up on end! The things I have seen here with my own two eyes, the sights I have witnessed! But then, the house has its secrets and I have to respect them, as its faithful retainer.'

I love this kind of talk, it sends delicious shivers of anticipation down my spine, it suspends my disbelief and so, conversely, ups the ante with my belief, in myself, my childhood, my life, who I am. At this stage I need more than anything to believe, and if I can believe Lohaniju, I can believe anything. His voice carries in it the residual texture of my childhood. I trust these stories in a desperate and vulnerable way, in the way, perhaps, that my boyfriend Anand had trusted me, before he chose to kill himself.

Anand had been another fictionaliser, he had wanted to be a novelist, or a film-maker, or perhaps a great dramatist. I have trained my mind to avoid thinking of him, of that purple jeering tongue, and I go through the set drill of forgetting. I put on my walking shoes and, covering my face with a muslin chunni, set off on a long walk. I go past the tennis court to the meadow where the marigolds bloom, to the spot near the stream which is my private refuge against the unexpected. I lie down on the damp earth and look at the sky above, and nothing has ever changed in my world.

I cannot sleep, I spend the nights reading. Yesterday – or was it last week – I rediscovered a cache of books from my childhood. Lohaniju found them for me. There was a heap of old comics, illustrated fairy tales, and a bundle of frayed and yellowed children's paperbacks. I was still hungering for a happy ending, so I devoured the fairy tales first, but I always abandoned them halfway. I wasn't ready for the bit where the Prince asked the Princess to marry him.

There was a book of poetry as well, an anthology, a collector's piece, probably, but I have put it away. I despise poetry. One day my least favourite student, Zenobia Desai, showed me a poem she had written. I was a little rough with her: I don't approve of adolescents writing poetry. It tends to fuck them up. 'You call this pathetic string of words a poem?' I asked, my face a perfect mask of disdain. 'I am afraid, Zenobia, that I can not allow you to waste my valuable time with your attempts at poetry. I suggest that you tear this thing up and turn your mind to less noble pursuits. Parnassus is not for you, my dear!'

'But, Ma'am, I've written it from the heart,' she exclaimed.

I lifted up my left eyebrow. (I could still do it in those days.) 'All I can say to you, young Zenobia,' I said, summoning all the sarcasm at my command, 'is to pay heed to Oscar Wilde's dictum.'

Zenobia looked at me mutely, an obstinate light in her gentle eyes.

'Do you know what Oscar Wilde said? "All bad poetry is sincere." Perhaps you should note what he said.' Dear God, what a pompous bitch I had been!

She stared back at me gravely, with that steady myopic gaze that never failed to infuriate me. 'You are probably right, Ma'am,' she replied, in a soft, almost inaudible whisper. Taking the sheet of paper back from me she proceeded to shred it into pieces right before my eyes. She did not tear it messily – she sheared it into long thin strips, which she held together and tore up yet again, crosswise this time. Then she went to the open window of the second-floor classroom and, in a rather silly and dramatic gesture, blew the torn-up papers off the palm of her hand and scattered them across the courtyard below. I had wondered then what the poem had been about, but of course it was too late to ask.

I sit at the window, gazing at the mountains, at the pine and the oak that surround us. Filling up these notebooks, listening to Lohaniju's stories, watching the day turn to dusk, awaiting the dawn. Another part of the drill is nail polish. Apart from my face, which I haven't looked at for a long time, I have resolved to be meticulous about my personal grooming. It's all too easy to fall into physical and emotional disrepair, I am not going to let that happen to me. I change my nail polish every two days. The ritual of the acetone and the cotton wool and the two clear quick strokes of colour is immensely reassuring. It works better than the tablets, which give me frequent headaches. I suspect that I am being over-medicated. I should telephone my sister and ask her to talk to the doctor who prescribed them.

Since my childhood, my sister has been my only ally. Her life, unlike mine, has always been safe, she errs only on the side of caution. It is comforting to know that the distance between us can be straddled by a telephone call, and yet I avoid calling her. I find that increasingly I have nothing to say.

The best time of day is the evening, when the sunset floods the room with warm orange light, and the polished surfaces of the old wood gleam with reflected fire. As I concentrate upon my nail polish my state of grace is complete; I inhabit the here and now of certainty and bliss. I study my well-kept hands with a sense of contentment and even achievement. Sanity is like nail polish: it chips easily, it has to be restored and renewed, and too constant a use can cause a yellowing of the nails.

While in hospital, recovering from the shock of the acid attack, from that hideous moment when Anand's sister had clutched my arm somewhere above the elbow and splashed the burning mess of hate and pain and unappeasable anger upon my face, after she had damaged and changed my life for ever, I had awoken from the dull flatulent half-life of anaesthesia, had flickered my still-intact eyelids, my curling eyelashes, had felt the tears drop to my cratered cheeks, and found myself in a room without shadows. The sterile light of the white hospital room looked unreal – without depth, plane or dimension.

What was real was terror and the stench of faeces from Anand's hanging body (the muscles of the sphincter losing control). What was real was unbearable pain: my skin and flesh and capillaries aflame with an unspeakable heat. Pain is a weak, inadequate word. It cannot speak of what happened that afternoon when the acid dripped from the beaker in that bitch's hand, her glass bangles clanking against the gold in her wrist, her nail polish, a bright pink, an innocent, impossible pink: her hand performing that unredeemable movement of mind and muscle, intent and momentum, and my face, my skin, my flesh, a surging writhing consuming mass of fire. I can still remember the sari she was wearing, it was a Dhaka Tangail 'Hajar buti', a thousand delicate motifs woven in pastel pink against the crisp, starched white cotton – did she plan that moment when she was pleating the folds of her sari that she would destroy me? Did she fasten the seal of her resolve as she snapped shut the little safety pin that held the pleats of her sari together?

In the flat light of my hospital room, of my clean white hospital room which still smelt of construction, my hospital bed which did not creak, this new environment so disconnected from the final moment in that month of insanity – in this room without shadows I felt contrition. Not regret at Anand's death – I hadn't killed him, of that I was sure – and not even anger at his sister's revenge. No, I felt contrition. Love, touch, joy, passion, the hard reality of my best friend's husband secure in my welcoming womb, the elation of being alive, of riding life – these were the culprits. I felt safe in that room without shadows: no harm could come to me there. My mind too yielded its recesses, its secret pockets of pain and hope and expectation, and lived for the one clean moment of inhalation and expiration.

My face had been banished from memory. Even in the bathroom they had taped up the mirror so that all I could see when I brushed my teeth in the mornings was a white sheet of paper that flapped faintly when the exhaust fan near the window (the barred window) was switched on. This was a new, fancy hospital, a plush and expensive hospital in the outskirts of Delhi, they were full of care and concern and newfangled ideas about the psychology of the patient.

*

After great pain, a formal feeling comes –
The Nerves sit ceremonious, like Tombs –
The stiff Heart questions was it He, that bore,
And Yesterday, or Centuries before?

Emily Dickinson, here in Ranikhet, in this bed which creaks, in the candlelight (the power has gone, a wire snapped, a pole fallen) with the insistent rhythm of the rain on the slate roof and a world of shadows closing in around me. I do not sleep at night; I am afraid of closing my eyes. I dread both dreams and reality but most of all I dread the half-light of that moment when one is not yet asleep, when the realities of night and day interlap, when the will is suspended and unreason begins its reign.

As a child, I was never afraid. My sister would whimper and cry at the slightest excuse or provocation, but I possessed a secret, hidden pool of resilience and belief that lay submerged somewhere between my mind and my young bodyscape, which I could access at will. As I grew older I forgot the way to this dream pool, and then, finally, it dried up. Now the shadows overtake me.

During the nights, I am possessed by the most dreadful sense of urgency, and the gentle eyes of our old *Bhotiya* dog, Lady, light up the dark that fills my room and save me from drowning. It is Lady's persistent breathing that keeps me sane through the nights, the kinetic nights when words and phrases from my childhood crowd the room, illuminating faces I can remember but do not recognise. It is on such nights that I put on the lights and count the rafters (there are forty-two of them) and blank out those memories which still flit between the shadows.

My uncle in Bangalore had bought the house when we were very young. My sister and I had played in the garden in the summers, we chased the butterflies, plucked the hydrangeas, killed wood beetles and buried them near the stems of the climbing roses that clambered over the veranda. When evening fell and the shadows lengthened we would retreat into the security and safety of the house.

An Englishman who had never lived here had sold the house to my uncle in an inordinate hurry. Lohaniju came with it: Lohaniju who told us stories; Lohaniju who held us tenderly when we stumbled on the steps or were stung by the nettles that grew high and wild on the tennis court.

There is a young girl in my memories, she is thin and shy, she is hiding behind a curtain in this very bedroom, behind the curtain in her parents' bedroom, and as she watches them fornicate, as she watches them at their loveless joyless task, her mother's eyes heavy with resentment, she feels someone else watching them with her. She does not know who this is, but it is a calming soothing presence, it holds her hand, it gently strokes her forehead, it instructs her to shut her eyes and pretend nothing has happened. When she shuts her eyes she can see a garden in bloom, a sweet-smelling garden in which a beautiful woman in a blue dress is walking, holding an enormous bouquet of flowers. It is the garden outside this house. When she opens her eyes again her mother is tugging at the drawstring of the petticoat she wears under her sari, and the girl waits until they have left the room before she emerges from her hiding place. I suppose that girl was me.

I remember that after they had left the room and I crawled out from my spot behind the curtain, I found a sparrow searching for an elusive morsel on the polished wooden floor. Motes of dust danced in the sunbeams as the sparrow looked up enquiringly, not in the least intimidated, I felt for a moment happy and complete and without a care in the world. The curtain moved and rustled in the breeze. I was brushed by a tangible presence, by a whisper of consolation and comfort, a dim consciousness which haunted memory yet evaded recognition.

I am sleepy. I am tired. The shadows are lengthening as the candle sputters in its earthenware stand. The electricity has failed; it often does in the evenings. I can hear the wind as it provokes the dark green needles of the deodar tree, I can hear it wail through the house as it rises up the chimney – I hate these sounds. When I shut my eyes I can see Anand's sister's face contorted by an expression which is beyond anger or hate or spite. If you asked me to describe her expression as she hurled the bottle of acid upon me I would call it 'playful'. I keep my eyes open to shut out the image of this face from my mind: it tends to float up in my interminable hours of half-sleep. I busy myself with other occupations: I play solitaire, I knit, I redo my nail polish, and as a last resort I count and recount the rafters. Today it is not her face that floats up before my eyes, but another one, a face without a face, a suggestion of a face, familiar yet mocking.

When at last I succumb to sleep I encounter the face again, but this time I recognise it, I know this person. I ransack my mind in the early hours of the morning trying to figure out who it is. 'You are a neurotic wreck,' I tell myself, but I'm not imagining it: that face is there waiting patiently to unmask itself. The next morning, as I brush my teeth, I evade my face in the mirror as I normally do, but there is a new dimension to my horror and repugnance, for it has struck me that the face I see in my dreams is really my own.

*

We have had a succession of *Bhotiya* dogs, all of them called Lady The '*Kukuriya baghs*', the dog-eating panthers, prey on them constantly. Lohaniju is a creature of habit, he likes to have a dog around the house and, according to him, it is a nuisance and a waste of time to keep on changing their names. *Bhotiyas* are the most wonderful dogs in the world, they are brave and fearless and loving, but they don't survive in the plains, they belong to these mountains, and in many senses these mountains belong to them. It's not just a charming inversion; there's more to it than that. This breed shares some symbiotic strength with the soil and stones of our mountains: *Bhotiyas* sanctify the places where they live. Forgive me if I sound sentimental, but these days Lady is one of my last links with the living world, it is she who keeps me sane. Being licked by her rough furry tongue is my only absolution from pain, my salvation, almost.

Lady's long black fur is tangled and covered with burrs. Her tail has the classic *Bhotiya* twist, and a speck of white at the end where it turns upon itself. I think perhaps I love this dog more than any of the other dogs that came before her.

The Doors again, it's that or Led Zeppelin. Perhaps I should switch to Lata Mangeshkar, to sweet saccharine sounds that can contain the pain.

Sometimes its difficult to tell music from sound. Music is sound syncopated by silence. Noise is messy.

I am not sure if the Doors are good for me, but they knew a thing or two about pain, that's for sure.

One night, as I was brushing my hair in the dressing room, I had a curious experience. I was overtaken by the sensation that my feet were not where I expected them to be. The ground below me had lost its authority, it no longer exercised the inevitable pull of gravity. The jute matting beneath me had abandoned faith and logic and assumed a life and form of its own. I felt weirdly disembodied; I was flailing, and my senses were overshooting themselves. It was as if I were receiving no information from my peripheries, as though my centre had been displaced. The fundamental and organic mooring of personality had completely abandoned me – I was as floppy as a ragdoll, but in the hands of what monstrous child I could not say.

My core felt different – it was as though I had been breached, as though someone or something had infiltrated me. I can remember quite clearly that my arms and legs began to go numb, and that there was a deep ringing sound in my ears. My voice when I spoke my own name out loud was hollow and suspect.

I remember awakening that night to find an iridescence suffusing the room. It was a circlet of light, like a gas balloon, or like ectoplasm, as I would imagine it to be from what I have read about seances and things like that. It wasn't fuzzy at the edges, but quite well defined, with a double-edged outline of orange and pink shaping its billowing luminescence. It hovered over the old desk that stood in the corner, it looked gentle and utterly harmless. I reached out under the bed for Lady's warm brown fur, and fell asleep again.

I dreamt of a woman standing in a garden, a bunch of summer blooms in her hand. I dreamt of a man in a cassock climbing uphill. When he turned to face me I confronted the deep empty sockets of his skeletal face. Yet I could sense that his eyes were sad, and that the grim contortions of his smile, of calcium and bared cartilage, were a travesty of his deepest emotions. I dreamt of deep night and a procession of fireflies. When I emerged from my night-consciousness I recalled these images with clarity and precision. I found they did not leave me or erode in my memory as the day progressed.

Lohaniju has showered me with gifts. The first apples of the season, misshapen, pocked with hail, not the over-red plastic imitations they sell in fruit shops in the plains. He has also brought me an old notebook, bound in green leather, bundled up in a decaying square of cloth which disintegrated when I untied it. Something in the book discouraged me from opening it, but read it I will, it's bound to be a change from the fairy tales I've been devouring.

When I asked him where he got it he looked mysterious, and his side-whiskers moved to indicate that he was smiling. 'There's a story behind it. After all, there's a story behind everything. I'll tell it to you later, when we light up the *sagad*, in the evening.'

We light the *sagad* in the evenings, to protect us from the cold. The draughty fireplace in my room has over the years lodged stones and leaves and even a family of owls. Lohaniju is too old to clean and repair it, so we have reverted to the traditional mountain system of heating: we burn pine-cones and cow-dung pats in the square, iron stove. Sometimes Lohaniju brings along a pocketful of chestnuts, which we roast in the glowing embers of the *sagad*.

Perhaps I am in much worse shape than I am willing to acknowledge at this point. The evenings set in early in our hills and, apart from Lady, it is only Lohaniju's comforting presence that prevents me from actually going bananas. I brought a music system with me when I came, and a bag full of cassettes and discs which are now scattered around my room. There is a lot of Kishore Kumar, which Lohaniju likes and even approves of, some violin and harp concertos and the sort of music which was popular when I was young, and which I discover is undergoing a revival – Led

Zeppelin, the Doors, the Moody Blues. My generation had listened to Abba and Kraftwerk, really, and preferred Asha Bhonsle to her sister Lata, but I was planning a dissertation on 'The Doors and the Poetry and Music of Doom'. It was either that or 'Popular Symbolism in Contemporary Hindi Films'. Anyway, I had Kishore Kumar on that evening, and the smell of roasting chestnuts. I even lit some candles on the mantelpiece above the fireplace; it gave the room a festive look, and Lohaniju and I settled down for the evening's revelries.

At first we enjoyed the music creeping about the room, searching out corners and eddies of silence. As the years pass, the joys of familiarity become increasingly important. The old book re-read, the story told for the umpteenth time on the same inflection of suspense, the music where one can anticipate the chords that are to come: one takes comfort in these things. Lohaniju launched into one of my favourite childhood stories. It's a poem, really, not a story, a poem written in Pahari which Lohaniju was fond of declaiming with total dramatic effect. It goes something like this:

Para gharua bhoot roon
je chan ch saboot duen

Translated that reads: 'There is a ghost under this roof. Do you want to list the proofs?' and so on. It's quite jejune really, with dancing skeletons and a rain of stones on the roof of the house and things like that, but it always managed to terrify my sister: probably because she is a cautious person; she needs to believe in the safety of her own habitation.

I listened patiently to Lohaniju, to indulge him – but then, he was reciting the poem to indulge *me*. Kishore Kumar was still crooning on, the Hindi film music so immensely reassuring by its very familiarity, and we had both forgotten for a while the unnameable burden which sat upon me when we were disturbed by a loud, indeed violent, hammering at the front door. Nobody ever comes to this house, so we were both surprised by the intrusion.

Lohaniju rose awkwardly on his long legs and hurried out to see who it was. The lights went off – it happens almost daily in our hills – and I contemplated the last of the embers in the iron *sagad* before me. Lohaniju returned after a while, shaking his head in puzzlement. There was no one at the door, he said, as he hurried away to get my supper. He had cooked potato curry and rice for me, and opened a can of baked beans, which he had garnished with onions and green chillies. Then he returned to the servants' quarters, which are a little distance away from the house, leaving me alone with the shadows, our *Bhotiya* dog Lady my sole companion and guard.

I lay in the bed in the dark room, shivering slightly even under the heavy quilt. The room was lit by three candles. Here on this isolated hilltop, it is easy to forget how close we are to tourist traps like Nain Tal. The gift candles which sputtered in the draught from the chimney had been bought by my sister in Nain Tal the last time she was there. One of them was particularly hideous. It was shaped like a naked woman, draped for the sake of modesty in some sort of flowing indeterminate garment. The candle was half spent, and the wax that had shaped her head shuddered and trickled down her torso, like some mutilated corpse set afire by a murderer. I wanted to blow it out, but the inertia that governs my life asserted itself and held me back from the effort and the physical co-ordination of the actual act.

Somehow I gathered the volition to get out of bed and snuff the candle out. It did not go easy into the good night, it continued to burn despite my efforts. Finally it yielded to my death wish. The room became darker. The smell of acrid smoke and angry wax filled the room. It smelt like murder. I had to erase this morbidity from my mind, I had to recondition myself. I would listen to music: Led Zeppelin, David Bowie, Jethro Tull. Anything. I fumbled for the battery mode, and inserted a new tape from the heap before me.

If music be the food of love, play on;
Give me excess of it, that, surfeiting,
The appetite may sicken and so die.

Eng. Lit. again. That villain Shakespeare and the unvanquished tongue of the conquerors. I had taught *Twelfth Night* once to a classful of giggling teenagers, in that long-ago place and time, that person I had once been. Where was I?

Led Zeppelin and *A Stairway to Heaven.*

The tape whirred ominously, as if it were hurtling to a precipice, or to that point in a waterfall beyond which there is no return. There were some clicking sounds, and then a man's voice filled the darkness in the room. '*That's just what I was saying!' he said, '. . . that's exactly what I was saying. The trouble with you is that you don't bother to listen to me. The trouble with you is that you are so bloody self-obsessed. You are conceited, you are vain, you are frivolous. The trouble with you is that you are you.*'

All our quarrels had been without reason, without focus. Anand had loved me for precisely the same reasons that he hated me. What was I to do?

I cowered under the quilt. I was abjectly afraid. I knew that voice. I recognised that voice. It was my fiancé Anand, my dead fiancé Anand, my dear departed fiancé who had been gracious enough to remove himself from our corrupted world to some nobler sphere.

I remembered that quarrel. It had been a wine and candlelight evening. I had invited him to my flat in Delhi; I had engineered the atmospherics to charm the soon-to-flower genius I had fallen in love with. Anand had been younger than me, twenty-six to my thirty-three. It wasn't only the arithmetic that was wrong.

Somewhere along the way the evening had turned sour, rancid. I had been wearing a red sari, a deep red sari. He had thrown a glass of white wine at me. I was so livid that I was radiating heat and anger, and I was actually grateful for the cool feel of the wine. Then Anand had taken a pin, (a pin, goddamn it!) from the desk where my students' earnest uncorrected tutorials and term papers lay, and pricked his finger with it.

Anand had taken the pin and carefully pricked his finger. A tiny droplet of blood, as red as my sari, oozed out of his skin, his living breathing skin. He placed the drop of blood upon my forehead, between my eyebrows, just below my bindi. I could feel his fingers. I could feel them here, now, in Ranikhet, in this house.

The voice continued to insinuate itself into the distant quiet, into this place where Anand had never been, and can now never visit. This, then, is what a ghost is: a voice trapped in time, startled from silence, displaced by accident.

The sound of crashing glass. Shattered. The glass pane. His hand, dripping more blood. He was always unstable. More fool me.

And then suddenly Led Zeppelin returns to the force field, and Anand is re-consigned to limbo. To the special hell reserved for successful suicides. Perhaps they read their awful adolescent poetry out loud to each other there. In the hell reserved for successful suicides.

I can feel myself choking. There are lacerations on my throat, the pressure of rope against skin and bone and cartilage. I can't breathe I am choking.

No, I am not afraid. I am not guilty. It is not my fault that I am me.

I sleep the sleep of the dead. No guilt, no remorse. I awake again as the first light of the morning creeps into the room. The dawn chorus heralds the arrival of day. First a single tinny-voiced bird twitters a brave but not entirely musical welcome to the Sun God. Gradually more voices enter the fray. It could sound lovely if I was in the right frame of mind, but my head is hurting.

O Romeo, Romeo, wherefore art thou Romeo?

The past exercises a tenacious hold over the future; sometimes it tyrannises it into repetitive patterns. I had come to the hills to obliterate my past, to seek refuge in the immediate present. Here was my past stalking me again, leaping out of a Led Zeppelin tape like a jack-in-the-box, like a practical joke gone sour. My instinct tells me to lie low, to evade discovery, to await the return of strength and continuity.

I shall busy myself in the ordinary. I will go for walks, and read, and paint my nails red. I will wait for these clouds to pass, these shadows to retreat. I have started on the old journal which Lohaniji has given me. The paper has aged only slightly, it is still crisp, and the ink has not faded at all. The handwriting, in spite of its old-fashioned flourishes, is in a simple running hand, and not in the least difficult to decipher.

There is something unnerving about this encounter between civilisations, the terrain is too immediate. Perhaps this is not what I should be reading, it is only reinforcing my paranoia. Yet I cannot help but be delighted by the density of the prose, by the detailed descriptions of the house and how it was built. It is a contradiction of my situation, and of many other academics, that we have to write and study a language which is not primarily our own. An adoptive and imitative idiom hinders the sensibility. This romantic encounter of an old-fashioned English prose style with our mountain landscape is all the more refreshing because of the uncanny circumstances of its retrieval. I can just picture Fanny sitting here in this house, so far away from home and all that was familiar to her, with the monsoon rains beating down on the slate roof for days and days on end. The house hasn't changed much, it's still just as the diaries describe it. Its like a time warp, this house set in the thick of an enchanted forest, this house that doesn't let you go.

II

THE INDIAN JOURNAL OF
WILLIAM JAMES COCKERELL, MA

As the hot weather of 1868 came on, we left Lucknow to begin a new mission at Rannee-khet, some twenty-two miles north-west from Almorah, in the Kumaon Himalayas. Mrs Cockerell had found the excessive heat in the plains taxing upon her already delicate nerves, and was glad to move to more opportune climes, nearer to the remembered environs of Home!

Kumaon is a sub-Himalayan region, 5,000 to 9,000 feet above the level of the sea. The climate is delightful – warm, but not oppressively so, in the summer, with the winters not as severely cold as in the land to which we were born. The rains are very heavy, for as the monsoon clouds encounter the great wall of the Himalayan Massif, a continuous blanket of rain descends upon these mountains, unrelieved by sun or shine.

When we arrived at Rannee-khet there was not a single house at the site. The only Europeans were two engineers and a sergeant, who had been sent to open up roads and investigate the potential of developing Rannee-Khet as a hill station, a place of retreat and rest for our soldiers, a refuge from the violent heat of the plains.

With the exception of a little land cleared on one side, the country around was covered with forests of pine, oak and rhododendron, interspersed with meadows or 'bugyals' where the people of the valleys pastured their cattle. The few natives I encountered looked upon me with fear, unable to comprehend that I was no Government official, come to levy taxcs or extort work but a humble servant of God, come with good tidings from Him.

I had arranged through a fellow missionary to have a wooden house erected, but at the time of our arrival the work had only just commenced, and for the first six weeks we lived in a tent. It was midsummer, and the tent in the daytime was intolerably hot. The trees around us were chiefly pine and, although a pleasant breeze was provided for us in the evenings, they afforded little shelter from the blazing midday sun. Mrs Cockerell, being of a delicate constitution, found the heat excessively trying, and would sit during daytime by the banks of a nearby stream, her boots and corsets unlaced, reading aloud the poetry of L.E.L.

'The Improvisatrice' was a poem my wife had always eulogised, although the admirable Letitia Landon was no longer the literary rage she had once been. As Mrs Cockerell, my sweet Fanny, sat by the gurgling waters of that clear Himalayan stream, in a 'bugyal', surrounded by fields of white and yellow narcissi, their full fragrance flooding the senses as though in a faery-bower, I had to remind myself that the love of God comes before the earthly loves that chimerically bind our lives. Fanny was reading the poem aloud in her soft sweet voice:

I loved him, too, as woman loves,
Reckless of sorrow, sin, or scorn:
Life had no evil destiny
That, with him, I could not have borne! . . .
I loved, my love had been the same
In hushed despair, in open shame . . .

I have never understood the refinements of poetry, but if it made the burden of mission life lighter for my Fanny, if it provided her consolation from the cares and uncertainties of life in these hostile lands, nothing could give me more joy than to share its pleasures. She was a woman of refined tastes, and her every movement and action reflected her dignity and discretion. Truly, my years with my sweet Fanny afforded me nothing but joyous happiness.

The young village boy who waited upon us was instructed, through a combination of Sign language and the rough local dialect, as to the preparation of a cooling lemon squash, using the local lime-fruit, which I believe grows in abundance in these fields. The native Pahari lads are blessed with rude good looks and a rugged build that compares very favourably with the hunched, stooped, ill-fed specimens encountered in the plains of Hindustan. They are indeed fine examples of manhood, and polite and punctilious besides.

My wife's spirits improved greatly in that leafy glade, where, to my partial eye, she reclined like a wood-nymph or a faery-sprite, or, in these Eastern parts, like houri or pari from the works of Sir Richard Burton, by which, I may hasten to say, I imply nothing indelicate.

The tent in the daytime was intolerably hot, and I resolved to put up a small wooden booth, a sort of Folly or Summer House, for our daytime comfort. A Mussalman carpenter had been brought from Bazpore for this purpose. I demonstrated to him how to cut and plane the pinewood, and he hammered together a comfortable resting spot, from where we could hear the chirping of cicadas and the call of the hummingbird.

When we arrived at Rannee-khet it was of course the height of summer, and a pall of dust sat over the landscape. The far mountains danced in a haze of glimmering heat and, although I had borne a month's sojourn to Benares patiently enough last summer, sometimes I too would be tempted to unlace my heavy boots and sit besides my Fanny in that verdant glade, dipping my feet in the clear water of the stream, a book of poetry or philosophy open before me. But such latitude is not advisable for the missionary, who must ever, in an alien and heathen land, maintain some barriers of sobriety and dignity between himself and the native peoples. If he forgets this, know that he is lost.

The calling of a missionary is quite different from that of a minister requiring, among other tasks, a great quantity of harassing and perplexing secular work. The average career of service in India for most missionaries is very short, some returning very soon, and others after a few years. Those who return home in the prime of life are rightly expected to enter the list of the home ministry, but the work they have left and the one they are entering are so different that the mental habits acquired in the one are felt to be a poor preparation for, and often even an obstacle to efficiency in the other.

Whether they labour at home or abroad, ministers and missionaries have the same message to deliver, that of the redeeming love of the Lord Jesus Christ. As His servants, nay, soldiers, we are required to endure hardship with fortitude and endurance. Although I have never for even an hour regretted my youthful decision to give myself to Christ's work among the heathen races, I am but human, and therefore culpable. Maintaining my calling among a strange, unsympathetic, sometimes hostile people, speaking His name in an alien tongue, in an alien landscape, searching for his visage in the unfamiliar features of an alien physiognomy, I cannot but confess to moments of heartbreak and dejection.

Many were the times when it was only the companionship of Mrs Cockerell which rescued me from the brink of the abyss of despair.

Not infrequently, young men have gone out to India as missionaries with the firm resolve to survive as their native brethren do, living in the native fashion, sharing the trials and tribulations of their flock. Determined as they were to eschew what they mistakenly conceived as the undue indulgence of those who had preceded them, yet the experience of one hot season generally brought them to another mind.

Despite better counsel those individuals who have adhered to their resolutions have encountered failure of health, insanity, and even death. No better example of such folly strikes the mind than that of our friend Mr Acton of Bareilly, whose ill-fated mission was burnt to ashes last winter: whether by design or accident has never been properly established.

The extreme climate of the Indian subcontinent, is, in my opinion, inimical to the stable growth of civilisation. In the searing summer months, not a blade of green grass is to be seen, and the ground is scorched, scarred and baked. When the first rains arrive, all nature is transformed. The parched earth gives way to the richest green. After the downpour, the sun comes out in all its strength. Under the combined action of heat and moisture, every conceivable form of vegetation thrives vigorously, as, alas, does an infinite variety of pestilential insect life.

In Rannee-khet, these insects did not wait until the rains to manifest themselves. At the height of midsummer, which was, according to the natives, hotter this year than most, a pleasing parade of butterflies, belonging if I mistake not to the species *Vanessa cardui*, the familiar 'Painted Lady', danced and swarmed across the hills and fields. The buzz of the dragonfly and the drone of the bumblebee inevitably brought to mind the happy recollections of an English summer. As the evening fell and the lamps were lit in our makeshift tents, the surrounding pine trees sighed in collective sympathy as though soul-sick with memories of home.

There is a scientific doctrine, called the Doctrine of Signatures, which is founded on the belief that every natural substance indicates by its external character its innate qualities. The pine trees around our camping ground, known locally as 'chir' or 'chil', were not strong, happy, upright specimens, but rather contorted and compressed, as in a corkscrew, their curious shape giving them a most melancholy look. I personally am of the opinion that this crooked variety is caused often by the southern aspect of the land, but in this case their warped growth persists even in those tracts which face directly to the snow mountains and the true North.

The superstitious villagers consider these pines unlucky in the extreme, claiming that all manner of sprites and goblins inhabit the unfortunately shaped trees, and moreover that the lay of our camping ground is on the hump or spine of the mountain, where the positioning of permanent or *pukka* houses is sacrilegious to their way of thinking. They themselves construct their houses in a huddle around some cramped bazaar, or else their humble hutments of wood and stone cling to the contours of the mountain, like a Red Indian child to a papoose. On ridges like the one whereupon we plan to site the house, they build only temples to their bloodthirsty gods. But this ridge, I have heard it muttered, is a bad one; it has a resident spirit which is inimical to happiness or reason. These fantastic claims from a race of idolaters made me only the more determined to establish my point of view, to show them the power of reason, logic and good sense.

The pine or 'chir' appears to have the property of driving out all other vegetation from the tracts it occupies, and forests of these trees are usually interspersed only with scanty underwood of the smallest shrubs and bushes. This however was not the case at our campsite, for 'banj' and 'tilonj' and 'kharsu', all local varieties of oak, grow plentiful in the slopes beyond the stream. These, likewise, are convoluted in their character and appearance, and as the evening falls they give a dark and eerie feel to these forests.

After the rains, which continued interminably, confining us for weeks to our dank tent, we got down to the construction of a dwelling place. My wife's spirits had been completely dampened by the dull, gloomy weather, and she whiled away the days perusing the novels of, among others, the Brontë sisters, to whose work she was very partial. As for me, I could not help but reprimand her for what in all truth I consider an unsuitable activity for a missionary's wife. Novels breed idleness and iniquitous fancies, but my poor Fanny is so innocent of any evil that, even as I spoke, I felt keenly the injustice of my reproaches.

The local populace, of whom we had gathered together quite a raggle-taggle, were of a helpful nature and eager to learn the finer points of the task of construction. The people here have a character for industry, and, compared to the idle plainsmen, our hill men are considered diligent and painstaking. A gentlewoman of intelligence and perception once told me that the work of one single English servant was equal to the combined labour of thirty native servants, but in terms of sheer strength the native Kumaonees are not wanting. The women, in this respect, surpass their menfolk, for in addition to household work they cut and carry great loads of wood and grass.

I am given to believe that no small degree of immorality prevails among the hill folk. The people here are fair and ruddy, and there is occasionally something almost European about the colour and tone of their skins and the cast of their bodies, yet their way of life is lewd in the extreme. Although polyandry, which I believe prevails in some districts of the Western Himalayan range, is not prevalent in these parts, polygamy is not uncommon among those who can afford it.

In addition to the indurating effects of sin everywhere, the people of Hindustan have for centuries been drugged with pantheistic and polytheistic teachings. A regrettable aspect of progress is a dulling in the educated mind toward the concept and very spirit of evil. Oh that the nature of sin was not kept so much in the background! For the over-virtuous are constantly led into the danger of temptation by the very generosity of their natures. 'Get thee behind me, Satan!' saieth the Lord, but is it not a point of theology that it was the shining virtue of our Lord that drew the Evil One like a magnet in an attempt to tarnish His glory?

I has been my calling to spread the name of our Lord Christ in these heathen lands. It is an unfortunate fact that many of our countrymen, be they the servants of John Company or Her Majesty the Queen, scoff at the efforts of those like myself engaged in missionary work. They know nothing about our work, but look upon us as 'Good men engaged in a Quixotic enterprise'. Often have I heard the opinion expressed, that Hinduism is as suitable a religion for the needs of Hindus as Christianity is for us, and they cannot conceive why a person should leave one for the other, except for the most sinister of motives. I need not tell my Christian readers my response to such heresies!

I debated in my mind what order of priorities to pursue: whether it was more appropriate first to build a mission house, and then a dwelling place for myself and Mrs Cockerell, or the other way round. It struck me that while the task of converting the local population could well be done from within the walls of a simple brick or stone structure, a proper mission house must surely convey the full glory of Christ and his peoples, and so I decided to build a house for myself and Fanny in a pretty knoll a short distance from the spot where we had first pitched our tents, by the side of an exceedingly noble and gracious deodar tree.

The deodar tree, a sort of Himalayan cedar, is considered by the hill people to be a living divinity. The ancient and shocking temples at Jaugeshwar, ennobling as they do the human phallus, are surrounded by an even older grove of these selfsame trees. If ever a deodar tree is required for the construction of a temple or Royal palace, it is first venerated and worshipped for several days, and its permission sought for the sacrifice, before the people dare to cut it down and use the logs for timber. I myself would have been well pleased to use this excellent wood for the beams and rafters of my house, but my instructions to this purpose were met with horror and outrage. I realised that, given the superstitious nature of these heathen souls, I could well have a mutiny on my hands. And so I chose to humour their respect for the tree-divinities.

I had arrived at a careful estimate of the costs involved. As the stone and wood required had to be carried on the heads and shoulders of native labour, we were obliged for the most part to use the wood and stone nearest.

Good building stone can be procured in most parts of Kumaon. Mica-schist forms the hill beds in these areas, and is not to be excelled for durability. At Rannee-khet, a pale coloured gneiss forms both a handsome and a lasting building stone, having the property of hardening by exposure. Our native friends were most helpful in the procurement and transportation of the stone, and a steady supply of even-sized building stone began accumulating at the site of the construction. I showed the men how to stack the bricks in a tidy and orderly fashion, and side by side with this activity commenced the digging, to establish strong foundations for the house, under the supervision of Areef Erfan, the Mussalman from Bareilly, who was also invaluable in prospecting for suitable wood.

It is the disability of the native mind that, in whatever sphere of concern, it does not have a sufficient regard for the foundation of things. The immediate nature of their concerns, and indeed the very nature of their religion, does not allow for any real contemplation of the hereafter. A lasting edifice is not built without a deep and serious foundation, and the mere gratification of greedy desires by praying to monkey gods and suchlike extends, among other spheres, to their architectural concepts.

They could not comprehend my insistence upon digging deep into the soil to establish firm foundations, and I could hear them scoffing at me in their rough native dialect, with which I had now become passably familiar. Their other reservations, about the suitability from the point of view of their superstitions of our chosen spot, had been quite overtaken by the determined pace of work at which we were proceeding.

Meanwhile, a very satisfactory stockpile of construction material was building up near the site. There were constraints not only of the absence of artisans and skilled labour, but also of finance and transportation. I sent a 'Botiya' coolie, a migrant from the Tibet border who had joined our group of ragged workers, to prospect through the district for materials. These 'Botiyas', I have heard it mentioned, are the heirs of the soldiers of King Taimurlung, of the ranks who did not return to China and Tartar but settled here in these mountains. In the absence of any guilds or market place or established building industry, the prices and quality of materials varied from spot to spot, and indeed from day to day. The Botiya was an honest fellow, frank and straightforward in his countenance, and not inclined to scowl or cringe as the local workman were. I took an immediate fancy to him, and, priding myself on my sound judgement regarding human nature, decided to delegate to him those tasks which involved the purchase and transport of goods. His experience in trading and his astute knowledge of the local mines (for the Botiyas are essentially traders in salt and borax) stood him in good stead here.

Our trusty Botiya had requisitioned some hill ponies for our use. These are hardy and useful animals, clumsy, rough and small, but sagacious, strong, and very sure-footed and docile. They cost in the range of twenty-five rupees each, and are in my opinion a better bargain than our contentious and obdurate hill folk.

It was now the fair month of October, which in our hills is very different from an English autumn. The copious monsoon rains have enriched and rejuvenated the soil, and a verdant green blankets the hills. The heavens are deep and startlingly blue, a rich cobalt colour unknown in England. Against this backdrop rise the noble snow mountains of the Himalayan range, brilliant in the mellow sunshine; reminders to the human soul of the pervading presence of God.

My fair Fanny was quite entranced by the sight, and by the masses of fragrant marigolds that bloomed in such abundance around us. She declared at once her ambition to embark upon a notebook of watercolours, to remember the pretty scene when we returned to England. In this she was hampered by the absence of paints or art materials, which omission I promised to rectify at the first opportunity.

We felt indeed that we were no longer in a dark foreign land, but in a sort of temperate paradise, where the clean mountain air and the pure sounds of birdsong proclaimed the proximity of the Divine. The mountain air in these seasons is invigorating in the extreme, and my dear wife developed a becoming ruddiness in her wan cheeks, and an unaccustomed sparkle lit up her lustrous eyes. She said to me, in her artless and unaffected way, how she fancied indeed that we were the First Man and Woman on earth, in the Garden of Eden before the Fall of Man. I cautioned her laughingly against the fancy, for much woe came to mankind from that primitive paradise, and Eve herself was responsible for the Fall. Whereupon she informed me that I was a pedantic and pompous gentleman, but she liked me very well despite that.

As for serpents, our Eden was certainly not short of them. Fortunately, for the most part these were harmless rat-snakes or grass-snakes whose voluptuous presence and sinuous movements could startle one in the most pleasant and unexpected of moments. There were, I was informed by Captain Ramsay himself, some exceedingly dangerous species of snakes, such as the krait, deceptively sluggish in its habits but deadly venomous when aroused, and the Halys Himalayan, more common on the slopes around Binsar than in Rannee-khet. This last personage, I was told, one must be extremely cautious about encountering: distinguished by a blackish band which proceeds from the eyes to the gape, it is a veritable messenger of death, much feared and venerated by the hill folk.

For these hill folk have a curious custom, not unknown in the plains, of worshipping and venerating the reptilian order of invertebrates. Whether, in the primitive nature of things, fear generates this respectful attitude, or whether there are some garbled superstitions coupled with the old wives' tales, I cannot say. Our rugged hill men informed me, quite seriously, that they would never harm or kill a 'Naga' (the local word for snake), for in it is contained a divinity which, when properly propitiated, could lead them to an immense wealth of gems and buried treasure.

My training as a missionary had taught me not to laugh outright in their faces, so I chose the opportunity to inform them, quite subtly, about the moral dangers of such material temptations, and to tell them the tale of Adam and Eve and the Fall of Man.

I instructed the workers to uproot and clear the numerous copses of hill bamboo that grew around our tent and in proximity to the construction site, for I had been given to understand that the bamboo usually harboured in its roots all manner of serpents. In this task they did not demur, but stubbornly refused to hurt, maim or kill any viperous pests, should they encounter them, however great the danger to themselves.

I must confess that they tried my patience sorely with their infinite procrastination. 'So-and-so was unwell, and so-and-so had fallen from a tree, or down a ravine or *khud* while chasing a cow, or contracted a fever' – ever it was the same tale. The hill folk are hard-working and enthusiastic enough when they get down to work, but when they abandon themselves to diversion it is well nigh impossible to rein them back to a steady rhythm. Their womenfolk are more dependable, and, sturdy and cheerful, often came to my rescue when the men folk were otherwise occupied, in the Devil's work.

My Botiya coolie had not yet returned from the mission on which I had assigned him, but I often found his sister, cheerful and pleasant as himself, at work at the construction site. Unlike her brother, who was dark-coloured and rather hideous in appearance, the sister was fair, with red cheeks and a suntanned complexion. She had, moreover, the most piercing eyes, with finely arched eyebrows. One eyelid drooped shut a little more than the other, giving a comical roguish expression to her countenance. She had, as did others of her race, a frame capable of endurance and agility, and she could lift the most awesome loads upon her strong back with a lithe and easy grace. It crossed my mind that she might make a very suitable maid-of-all-work for my dear Fanny, and I resolved to talk to her brother about it upon a suitable occasion, when he returned from his mission . . .

Now this Botiya girl, whose name was Lali, began troubling my consciousness in strange ways. Whenever I was at the construction site she would follow me about with childish enthusiasm, like a playful puppy, quite oblivious to the reprimands of the other natives, who were more conscious of the divide between our respective positions. We are of course all equal before our Maker, yet Lali carried in her every movement an unhampered unquestioning freedom; she was a pagan to the core.

One warm afternoon, when my Fanny lay in the tent, a cold towel upon her temples, a book of poems by her bedside, I decided to go for a walk in the woods beside the stream. My spirit was troubled; I was puzzled and perplexed by the nature of my duties, and the burden that God had laid upon me, here in this distant land. In these hills nothing that is true or good is worshipped. Their heathen gods are subject to bargaining and religious bribery. Magic, the Black Arts, and the most evil, depraved and corrupt forms of the Tantric cults are given prominence in their creed. The local people have abiding faith in inert or material articles, in ghosts, goblins and ghouls. A God who is good is near-incomprehensible to these wretched races; but so-called deities who destroy the life and property of people by deceit, and cause fear and pain, are honoured and respected.

Sometimes, God forgive me. I have wondered if these shapes and forms that walked and laboured and laughed around me were even human, or only shadows belonging to some other, unchastened, unchristian world. I wondered if it was only my pride that possessed me to consider myself superior to them; they lacked no earthly joy, and of the other world we have, after all, only promises. Thus doubting, I wandered about the slopes around the tent, as the mountains glimmered white and distant to the north and the blue sky mocked the terrors of my mind.

Even the clear, clean water of the stream seemed to laugh at my questionings. 'What?' it seemed to ask. 'What what what what what what?' The marigolds bloomed in sweet contentment, and the pastoral quiet of the scene led me to lay my head down and seek refuge in the green lap of the earth. Imagine my surprise when I felt behind me the form of another human, and Lali, she of the roguish look and charming smile, assaulted me violently, like an animal; a beast, even.

She tore open my cravat and unclothed me before the blue sky. I resisted her with all my might, but she howled and shrieked like a Fury and pursued me with all the more vigour for my resistance. I am an honest man; I will not say that I was not aroused. There is an animal within each of us, and the calling of the missionary is to subdue and tame this animal. But here the animal was pursuing me; it sought my soul. The grunts and shrieks and rapacious murmurs with which she assaulted me shame me even today, but by the help of God I resisted her. My refusal seemed only to excite her the more; and then, before my eyes, she got up and ran like one possessed, waving the sharp scythe which the hill women carry always about her head in a dreadful death-dance.

There is a point to the west of the field beside the stream where the undulating slope falls suddenly to a deep dark ravine. It was to this point that she ran, lashing and whipping herself with her scythe, leaving a trail of blood in the green grass and the marigolds. And then with a dreadful dying call she leapt off the ravine and plunged to her death in the abyss below, decapitating herself with one fell swoop as she plunged.

Not in Africa, not in the wilds of New Guinea, not in the safe comfort of my home in England have I ever forgotten that sight, that sound! It was a sound of neither sorrow nor rejoicing: it arose from somewhere deep within her, an extraordinary and elemental sound, a ululation such as intersperses the acts of the Greek tragedies. Then came that vision of death and destruction that I have tried all my remaining life to obliterate from the press of memory, the sight that will hound me until the last sigh leaves this accursed unfortunate frame!

There was a sound of drums, of the local *Damru* and *Hurkia*, the hand-held drums these natives favour, and then a strange procession entered that tranquil field from the bend of the hill. An enormous 'dandi' or palanquin, too large for the use of any ordinary mortal, came into view, followed by a pack of dogs of a size and shape I had never before encountered. The dogs, dozens of them, were running through the marigolds, and yet the flowers were neither bent nor crushed. Small bells had been tied like collars around the necks of these dogs; a strange tinkling, a clear crystalline sound not of this world, filled the air. The attendants, who carried upon their emaciated shoulders the burden of that outsized palanquin, were murmuring and whispering a strange song, the words of went as follows: 'Sau, sau, sau, sau, sau!' Two women followed the palanquin: their legs were twisted and their faces turned backwards. They were dancing a wild, wanton dance. Behind them were two more women, beautiful beyond the dreams of mortal eyes. They were humming and singing a mysterious song; and this song was accompanied by glad gesticulations and gay movements. And then, before my astonished eyes, the procession of spirits vanished into the air, and all was still and silent again.

The next day talk was heard in the village that the God Airee, whose temple it is rumoured once stood upon the peak of this hill, had seen fit to visit his people. These visitations by Airee, I discovered, are dreadful events that bring in their wake death, despair and dishonour: few live to see Airee and tell the tale. I told no one but Fanny of what I had seen; neither did I consider it appropriate to mention the circumstances of Lali's death. Not only would it give credence to their village superstitions, but it might further be misrepresented to malign and dishonour a man of the cloth and the sacred message of our Lord. I kept silent, but there are no secrets in the hills, and I felt that the eyes of the natives wore a knowing, mocking look.

'Who knows what evil lurks in the hearts of men!' There were murmurings among the hill folk, but none dared question me about the matter, not even Lali's brother. After she was discovered to be missing, her friends and kinsmen began a search for her. Her mangled body was at last found at the foot of the ravine where she had leapt to her dreadful death. The head had already been carried off by wild beasts. After disposing of her body through a fire ritual, and burying her silver 'Hansuli' necklace in the ground, as was their custom, her brothers and kinsmen congregated to mourn Lali's death. For this purpose they slaughtered a goat and consumed vast quantities of rice and wine and meat. For three days they were in a wild state of intoxication, in honour of her memory: the beat of drums and the sound of brawling could be heard even at the site of our tent.

The villagers, whose superstitions I had hitherto mocked, said Airee was angered and so a demon had possessed Lali: that she had been the victim of a malicious goblin that prowled often and betimes in these parts. They exonerated me of any ill intentions, for they knew that I was an honourable man. Yet my spirit was shamed and my faith humiliated, my mind was racked with guilt and despair, my eyes forever imprinted with the awful scene.

My dear Fanny could not withstand the shock; her fragile health and frayed nerves could not bear the upheaval in our innocent lives. She was brave, and strong, and never questioned me about the strange episode. Indeed she stuck to her resolve to 'paint a picture of the pretty scene', depicting the blue sky and the field of marigolds. Yet she went into a rapid decline, her blue eyes were hollows in her lovely face, her delicate hands those of a living skeleton. The villagers were now more than ever reluctant to proceed with the construction, saying that the spot was bad, that evil spirits resided and revelled there. In despair I brought in a new work-force of Mussalmans from Bareilly, to work under the direction of Areef Erfan. The house was built, and Fanny and I moved in within the year. We furnished it as best we could within our humble means. Fanny's watercolour hung upon the wall, a pretty and innocent picture, depicting the stream and the marigolds blushing under the blue sky.

My dear Fanny would insist that she could glimpse some kind of sprite or apparition in the house. It told her kind tales, soothed her aching brow, and behaved with decorum and consideration. I beseeched her to abandon such fancies, for they do not behove the wife of a missionary. To which she replied with the passage from Corinthians:

So also is the resurrection of the dead.
It is sown in corruption; it is raised in incorruption.

Well pleased with this evidence of her reading something besides the dreadful fictions to which she was addicted, I did not dispute the matter further.

I continued with the work of the mission, but the state of my dear Fanny's health caused me much anxiety. She would sit before the draughty fire in the upstairs bedroom, her eyes rolling as though she was viewing strange visions. I would seek to soothe and comfort her, but to no avail. Outside, the mountains mocked our enterprise, and the wind whispered deceits upon my ears. Before the year was out I laid my Fanny to rest, her dear eyes shut in eternal sleep.

It is sown a natural body; it is raised a spiritual body.

I have pondered the wisdom of writing these journals; memory is capable of delusion, and the mind of man falls prey to many fancies. I know in any case that my journals will never see the light of day. As I sit, old and tired, in an England now forever alien to me, surrounded by fragments of memory, I fear for my own sanity. Better to forget!

The memories of that house and the time I spent there haunt me to this day. I shall go there again, I shall return to Ranee-khet, to that same spot in the mountains, and confront the past. There is no other way.

I tell this sordid story only as a cautionary tale to my brothers of the cloth: of the dangers and deceptions of strange races, of the abominable practices prevalent in heathen lands, the dangers that the best of men are prey to in the pursuit of their mission. Heed, or heed not, it is your will.

I have heard Satan laugh!
My house is founded upon a lie!
God knows I meant well!

I.ii

. . . when you have eliminated the impossible, whatever remains, however improbable, must be the truth.

Sir Arthur Conan Doyle, *A Study in Scarlet*

I am being stalked. I know I am being stalked. All the evidence is there – all the telltale signs of a . . . person? entity? stalker? . . . intent on pursuit. Every time I turn my head I see the shade of someone hurriedly retreating – there is a suspicious silence which follows my silences like a pause. I don't like it. I am afraid. It is not my imagination, there are things I see, words I hear which are outside the sphere of any experience I have ever had.

The house has begun to speak to me. I do not want to listen to its stories, they are malicious and convoluted. At least the rain has stopped. Drip, drip, drip on the slate roof – it was driving me insane. Now the clouds have gone, there are no more banks of fog rolling into the house and making things even more spooky. Perhaps it is time for me to leave, to return to the city, to my job. But I don't know if I can ever return: isolation feeds on loneliness until one day you realise you just can't face anything any more.

'You just can't face anything any more.' That's both apt and ironical, I guess. I glimpsed my face by accident in the mirror the other day, and I literally reeled from the shock. The planes of my face have changed, and there is a raw look about it, which makes me cringe. I take refuge in painting my nails. At least my hands are still as beautiful as they ever were.

*

The worst of the monsoon is over: at last the weather is beginning to clear. It's a relief to be able to see the snows again. I had forgotten how beautiful the Himalayas were, Chaukhamba and Nanda Kot and Trishul, proud and inaccessible, serene in their solitude. I sit in the balcony much of the day, or by the window in my room, and watch the changing colours of the snow peaks. Nothing matters at those heights, the air is not designed to support life, only to deny it. When people die of altitude sickness they enter a mode of alternate reality, nothing engages them, they don't even know or care if they are dying. I wonder if Shivji really lives there, under Mount Kailas. Lohaniju assures me that he does, serpents and all. I asked him, just as a joke, where Parvati went to get her sexy little cholis tailored, and he fell into a rage, a real rage such as I had never witnessed before. He said I was half-educated and suspended between two worlds, like Trishanku. Since I didn't have the good sense to hang on to my beliefs it was unlikely that my beliefs would stick on to me, that was what was meant by the destruction of *samskaras*, the breakdown of values.

He sulked for a day, and so did I, and then we made up the next morning. He must have been quite lonely in this house before I arrived. He has no family living with him, although he has a daughter who is married in a nearby village. She visits him sometimes, she brings him fresh cow's milk in a shining brass lota, and she offered to knit a sweater for me if I bought her the wool.

I sit in the sun a lot, my skin has turned a deep brown and my hair is a bronze-gold colour. I re-read the diaries again. They document the progressive breakdown of a man who was probably not very sane in the first place. I am keeping a close watch on my own sanity, constantly alert to signs of collapse. Perhaps I have become too self-conscious. I find I am scrutinising myself all the time.

Perhaps I'm just trying too hard to be normal – it really is one of the stupidest things one can do. I tried too hard to love Anand, much too hard – if I hadn't tried so desperately to love him, none of this would have happened. I have to let go, before I can return to myself.

The word 'alienation' belongs to the context of psychopathology. All human beings harbour their particular and individual manifestations of the Other. In the widest sense, every neurosis is the outcome of some form of alienation. But why am I even writing all this? Clearly, it's not me that's mad! Anand was crazy! I'm sure he had temporal lobe seizure the way other young men have girlfriends! His sister is crazy! I'm all right, I won't allow them to get to me, now or ever.

Let us forget the blind forces of the subcortex. Reality is fundamentally orderly. It has a pattern and a design. It also has its secrets – most of what is real within us is not conscious, and most of what is conscious is not real. Why am I babbling these big words? What am I running away from? Why am I afraid of the fiction of my rationalisations? Perhaps I should just submit to this alternate world. If I redo my nails – if I file them into perfect ovals and paint them pink (pink the colour of love rather than red the colour of violence) – if I paint them pink I might last out another day.

Watchman, what of the night?
The watchman says:
Morning comes and also the night.
If you will inquire, inquire:
Return, come back again.

I feel trapped in this house. Although I am living all alone in these eight rooms I feel crowded, I feel closed in by presences. The October air is very dry, and I am suffering from frequent nose-bleeds. My handkerchiefs are spotted with blood, and I feel faint and light-headed as a consequence. I have run out of anxiolytics, and for some strange reason there are none available in Ranikhet market. This sounds like a long list of trivial complaints, but the days are so short now, it gets dark by mid-afternoon and then I'm trapped in my room, with the shadows closing in.

Last night there was someone in my room. Even Lady could sense it. She cocked her ears, as though alert to some sound I could not hear. Her brown fur rose and stood on edge. A ridge formed upon the curvature of her back, and her trusting brown eyes seemed focused on some point near the fireplace.

I lay in bed paralysed with fear. Dry mouth, sweating palms, thumping heart and shallow, hasty breathing. My heart beat so hard that at each beat a loose brass knob on the bedstead rattled. When I woke up (although I don't know if I ever slept) my mind was blank, I was exhausted, and my one desire was to get away.

The past few days have gone in a haze. My only consolation is an old school arithmetic book. I spend hours and hours completing the simplest sums, taking delight in the certainty and predictability of the answers. Sometimes when I get the answers wrong, I fall into an even greater panic and attack the problem again, my palms sweating, my tongue dry, my fragile world destroyed.

My nail polish is chipped and I don't feel like repairing it. It's a grim scenario any which way you look at it – a promising young life nipped in the bud. I'm not talking about Anand, he did it to himself, if he chose to hang from a noose of rough jute rope he deserved what was coming. No, I'm talking about myself, Rachita Tiwari, touching thirty-four, forgotten as a person by the world, remembered only as a sensational story. Even Lohaniju knows me only as Bitiya. Although he is kind to me in the way the strong are always kind to the weak, I won't deny that there is a degree of humiliation involved in receiving his love.

When I was young my favourite writer was Enid Blyton. I was in love with Fatty, and with the English countryside, with muffins and scones and tongue sandwiches. I discovered a childhood book hiding in the bottom of the bookshelf on the landing by the staircase. It was called *The Mystery of the Invisible Thief.* My name was still written in green ink on the title page. The Five Find-outers had got it wrong, I reflected sadly. The invisible thief is time.

Giving voice to my own astonishment, I collapse and cohere in turns. Perhaps I will after all one day write a novel – I'll become an author, I'll write a bestseller and go for the launch in a black lace mantilla and have all the men in the audience wildly in love with me. Perhaps. Or perhaps I'll just live here for ever, and my sister will send me endless parcels of clothes and baked beans and Haldol, and I'll bury Lohaniju when he turns one hundred and dance on the grave. Of course, I'd kill him first. Ha ha.

Experience is the raw material of life. Life is the sum of our meagre experiences. A conundrum is a no-win situation. After a while it becomes easier just to drift. Yet anger can at least affirm, while regret redeems nothing.

Actually it's not as isolated here as it seems, Ranikhet is only a stone's throw away. We even had some picnickers here last week;

they left plastic evidence of their pleasures in the tennis court. I should have seen them from the balcony, but I didn't. Strange.

The students in my class sent me a Diwali card. 'Dear Ma'am,' it said, 'all the best for Diwali and the coming year. English Honours II.' Sweet. I guess. Smug little bitches with their smooth faces and unplaned brains. I could kill them for what I've lost.

The nights are unbearable. This house is crowded. The procession of horrors that invades my consciousness with monotonous regularity is wearing me down. I read a story in the newspapers a few years ago, about a man with a piece of shrapnel in his brain which became activated into a radio receiver. He kept picking up scraps of radio transmission all the time. That's how it is with me, I'm tuned into something I don't understand. I keep trying to trip myself up, to break into the rationale of these hallucinations, but I swear I do actually see them, they materialise and derealise like something out of a science fiction film.

Am I the perpetrator or the victim of this dream madness – do I inhabit these phantoms or do they inhabit me? Although I can still view things from the outside, I am irresistibly drawn into this internal and external disorder, this doubling of consciousness, I am still stunned by the speed and skill with which this seductive new world has breached the already frayed realities of my life.

Nothing connects. When I look at a book I see signs, symbols, strings of words. They do not flow into each other – they do not accommodate into order, they do not make sense. Chaos reigns. Everything has gone; only pain remains unvanquished, a raw constant pain that is almost a stimulus.

Nothing is what it seems to be. Even my arithmetic is dismayed. Mathematics is sanity, even when it moves towards increasing levels of abstraction. It battles change and disequilibrium. And now, these anomalies, these confusions. What is happening to me?

You could say that I have ceased to exist, become but a consecution of surreal perceptions, derelicted by spatial time and left at the mercy of a world suspended between unrealities.

Yet as we get more comfortable with each other, we have learnt to observe some of the fundamental rules of privacy. We are like people in a very crowded bus, towards the end of a very long journey. We sense and know our separate destinations, yet the journey which has thrown us together has knit a sense of intimacy between us.

In literary terms, the 'appropriation of voice' refers to the usurpation of narrative identity. That is the closest I can get to describing what it is that is happening to me. From somewhere beyond the curtain that divides their worlds and mine, these shadows are seeking my voice, appropriating my self. My definitions of who I am are coming undone, and yet I do not think I am going mad. Of course, that is what we all say.

I went out for a walk today. There had been a break in the monsoon, it hadn't rained for a while. The earth is still soft from weeks of unremitting downpour, it crumbles and falls apart at every opportunity. The snakes have been rained out of their burrows, and Lohaniju cautioned me from venturing out alone. 'Take a walking stick with you,' he said, 'tap it on the ground and warn the snake-world of your presence. If you take them by surprise they may be tempted to retaliate.' So here I am, a crooked staff in my hand, a muslin chunni over my face, a sight to scare children myself, off on a solitary walk to contemplate the startling beauty of the autumn hills.

Another gem of folk wisdom from Lohaniju. 'If you do see a snake, check if it has a *mani* on its crown. Many of the snakes here wear priceless gems, rubies, even diamonds, upon their foreheads. If a human gets hold of these gems, untold wealth follows them all their lives.'

'So I just grab it from the snake, this diamond or ruby?' I asked, quite seriously. I don't dare joke with Lohaniju.

'No, Bitiya, never grab anything. Just recite the magical spell – *Astika, Astika, Astika* – three times, no more, no less, and the name of the king of Nagas will compel them to obey you.'

Well, I did encounter a snake on my walk. There is a path that unfolds in the hill below the house, that winds around until you reach the stream beside the fields, and then back to the house again. There is a spot in that walk that I always felt was enchanted, privy to secrets, peopled by sprites or fairies or some such benevolent spirits. A copse of *banj*, of Himalayan oak, is clustered around a little waterfall that tumbles prettily to a clear pool surrounded by a heap of dolmen-like rocks. There was a forest of ferns around me, delicate cautious tendrils of the most heart-rending green. I sat down on a rock and contemplated the scene, forgetting for a while the confusing dilemmas of identity.

The trees above me were still drenched with the afternoon's downpour and a constant dribble of wetness soaked me from the oak leaves. The oak, the local *banj*, is not considered auspicious by hill people, it is the shelter of wandering spirits, the abode of wraiths and ghosts. As a child, I was forbidden to play with acorns: it was bad luck to bring them into the house.

As I sat on the rock, I realised that a green snake, probably a harmless garden variety, had made itself comfortable by my feet and was staring at me with an expression of intense curiosity. 'Astika,

Astika, Astika,' I murmured softly. To my surprise, I discovered that I was not at all afraid. I liked the fluorescent green of its scales, the same green as the fern. Something in the colour gladdened my heart; it perfectly complemented the grey of the low brooding clouds and the clear transparency of the water. Delhi seemed very far away, another world of dust and grime and vengeance.

I could have sat there for ever, but finally the snake disappeared into the ferns, leaving behind a glittering red object where it had been. It was a deep red stone, some sort of uncut gemstone. Perhaps it was a *mani* like the ones Lohaniju was always talking about. I put it into my pocket and decided not to walk any further.

It began drizzling as I turned back, and at a bend in the walk I found myself tripping over a branch of pine that had fallen on the path. As I stumbled and fell all I had to hold on to were the tall nettles that grew by the side of the path. I clutched at the nettle bushes to avoid falling on my face, and when I was upright again my hands, which had grabbed the stinging leaves for support, were not hurting in the least, as logically they should have done.

There was a lesson in that, a lesson I understood instantly. The nettles are the natural guardians of the mountains, they resist intrusion and prevent the soil they grow upon from being desecrated. A firm hold on anything, even reality, hurts less than a timid halfway encounter. Pain is a precondition to life, a prelude to joy. It is a teacher, not a tormenter. Lack of stimulation leads only to a lack of sensation. Better, then, the pain

Why can't I understand this in daily life?

The sad part was that I lost the stone. It fell out of my pocket when I stumbled and fell, and although I searched for it for days in a row, it was of course not to be found again.

*

I went to the bookcase by the stairs to look for something new to read. I needed to distract myself, to slide into this altered mode obliquely, as it were. I found an old volume of Mahadevi Verma's poems. Perhaps they had belonged to my mother. Or to my aunt. I had met Mahadevi Verma, here, in this house, many years ago. She was not in any sense a beautiful woman. It sounds cruel, but she looked as if she had acid thrown upon her face already. Evidently, even though my beauty has departed, my vanity has not.

Well, she was a plain-looking woman, with eyes that glowered at one from behind thick spectacles. I had been very young when I met her, and she had seemed very old – was it any wonder then that I found her grotesque, repulsive, alien?

It was only now, many years later, that I actually read her poetry. I could not at first connect the poems with that woman I had known, had seen and met in these hills all these years ago. Her poetry is beautiful, mystical, though perhaps a little abstruse.

The 'Chhayavadis' – Sumitra Nandan Pant, Nirala, Jayshankar Prasad, and of course Mahadevi herself – were self-acclaimedly poets of the shadows. They recoiled from the new realities of modern India and retreated into a regressive post-Romantic swoon. In short, they were all hopelessly silly – all moths and lamps and silent wilting ladies with tears welling from their luminous eyes: not my cup of tea. As I mentioned before, I hate poetry, I have always hated it. It is lying, deceitful, fraudulent. Plato was right to bar it from his Republic. I was completely justified in tearing up Zenobia's stupid outpourings, though I do confess I feel a twinge of guilt about that now, here in the hills, where I am becoming somewhat sentimental and swoony myself.

Perhaps I hurt her feelings. Who can tell, perhaps the poems were good. Well, it's too late now. Too late for anything.

Pain sticks to my mind
Like a damp cloth;
As though drowning, these wet sighs
Come crowding to my lips.

That's Mahadevi Verma. Poet of the shadows.

I'm not comfortable with Hindi, with the Devnagari script, and yet I am compelled to read these poems. I am drawn to them as a moth to the candle, to use the rather hyperbolic language and metaphor of Mahadevi Verma. After all, she too lived here in these hills, and indeed died here, in an old house facing the snow mountains.

In spite of Chaucer and Spenser and all the alien metatext that has been rammed down my throat by nuns and missionaries and well-meaning academics, Professors and Doctors of Literature who dream of Keats and poesy and Parnassus and all that spurious nonsense and eat dal and soggy chappatis packed by their tired wives in steel tiffin boxes at lunch before they resume their tryst with the tyranny of the English tongue, in spite of all these factors I find that I do recognise and understand Mahadevi's poetry. I understand it, I respond to it.

Mahadevi totally metaphorical activities exclude any hint of the real. This completely subjective play is peopled with elusive symbolic figures – the Woman, the Widow, the Beloved – depicted weeping, waiting, strumming the vina. This extended metaphysical conceit co-opts the private universe of abstracted emotions until . . . until . . . until I tear up these lying words, repudiate this nonsense, paint my nails a blazing scarlet.

She's hysterical but very, very good. As for the illustrations, they're in the old Bengal school of soulful portraiture, almond-eyed women with tapering waists and mermaid-feet holding lamps or lotus flowers in their elongated hands.

Mahadevi is a sort of camera obscura, the kind they had in the Middle Ages, which painters used to reflect the proportions of their subject. I cannot divine whether she is coherent or incoherent – I do know that, in the principle of like repelling like, she is able to distract me, to keep me sane, clear of the shadows. They are still intent on pursuit. If I do not hold out they will appropriate my voice, my inner resources of articulation and understanding. They need to subvert me, make me their own. What better defence against their attack than the voice of another, of a lonely woman poet who too has watched the shadows lengthening as the daylight abandons the distant heights of the Himalayas. Like my face in the mirror, Mahadevi is a reminder of the self I actually am.

In the bosom of the night I am the arrow of the day's desire.
Empty was my birth,
And the dawn is as a death:
Darkness alone the companion
Of my restless spirit.
Speak not of union: In separation I am eternal.

Carl Jung writes about synchronicity – an inner logic in the configuration of events. Reading Mahadevi's poetry seemed to have opened the door to another species of coincidence.

I discovered a prism lying in an old box in a drawer in the desk upstairs. When I looked through it, the world changed. Every reality got broken and translated into colour. One afternoon a very strange thing happened, strange even in the scale of the other strange things that were constantly occurring wherever I looked. Instead of the familiar and predictable range of violet, indigo, blue, green, yellow, orange and red to which I was routinely conditioned; a new colour appeared on my prism. It was a completely unexpected colour, a colour I had never seen before: amber is the closest I can get to describing it, but it was not amber, it was a composite of another range of vision altogether. As I observed my world bathed in that beautiful glowing light, as I saw the table and the chair and the fireplace refracted in this puzzling but entirely pleasing new reality, I felt somehow safe and secure and familiar, as though I was retreating or retiring to a place I already knew and recognised. I sat with the prism held close to my eyes, lost in the splendour and surprise of this new world. Everything was as it should have been, nothing around me had changed, but that glowing amber light conferred a mystery and glory on everything it touched.

I did not care if it was a trick of the vision or a detour of the mind. I knew that the light flowed from the prism to my eyes, although I could not tell if it actually flowed out again into the other world without. I remember looking out of the window at the Himalayan ranges, the joy and abandon of discovery in my eyes. It was a clear day, and the afternoon snows shimmered golden yellow as the dawn through my prism. The mountains seemed to be thrusting up, to be reaching out to the sky, to the valleys, breaking and breaching the boundaries of their mountain-ness and becoming part sky, part valley. Then I lost the prism, it just disappeared, it was not there in the desk or the drawer or anywhere in the house, although Lohaniju and I both searched for it everywhere.

Writing about it now, I feel an urge to describe that wonderful colour. It had a quality of light, it glowed, it had a consistency and depth which was somehow granular. Amber is perhaps not the correct word, amber is too orange – but I would not call it yellow. As I struggle to remember, I find the elusive glow fading from my mind, abandoning me even in memory, and I wonder, as I have wondered before, if it was all some demented hallucination, if I ever really saw that transfiguring colour at all.

Synaesthesia is a physical condition of the cerebral cortex that leads to a fusion of the mental and emotional worlds, of the abstract and the concrete in our perceptions. Many artists and writers, notably Rimbaud, have 'suffered', if that is the term for it, from synaesthetic visions of sound and colour – they have 'felt' numbers, 'seen' the colours of emotions, 'heard' flowers. Synaesthesia is, literally, a crossing over of the senses, a demolition of the internal boundaries and constraints that demarcate the territories of experience. I have heard and read about synaesthesia, perhaps I am now 'suffering' it.

The amber light was more than a light. It was a way of viewing. Sometimes I shiver from the very intensity of my visions, my hair stands on end and I am rocked by an overflow of the senses.

I can see beyond the curtain. I know there is someone there, some thing that will surely claim me one day. Resistance is useless.

III

Let the new faces play what tricks they will
In the old room, night can outbalance day
Our shadows roam the garden gravel still
The living seem more shadowy than they.

W.B. Yeats

The house had been empty for a long time, though a few people had come and gone. Dona Rosa sat at the bay window, watching the sun set over the Himalayas. She had the most serpentine mind I had ever encountered, and even as I tested the waters I got a charge, a powerful rush from the sheer flow and energy of her being. She was brushing her hair, the brown hair that came tumbling to her shoulders, her curly brown hair that seemed to assume a life of its own as she massaged it with her fingers before resuming the steady rhythm of sure mechanical strokes with the hog-hair brush which she held like a weapon in her lovely hands. She had the peculiar concentration of a beautiful woman lost in self-homage, and I decided that I liked her and that I would give it a try.

I hide in corners, I lurk in shadows You might glimpse me, behind the corner of a smile, or in the set of the eyes, sometimes. Getting in is easy, but they are so very boring, most of the time, and infiltrating a human involves getting trapped in a time dimension as well. There is no end to it then, linearity prevails, and day follows day, and they do so little with their lives. You can excite them, incite them to mischief, but after a while it's all more of the same. I have always fancied the contemplative life myself, I like silence, and pauses, and I sense that if I could defuse my force-field I could find the exit I have been seeking for so long.

But I liked this woman, I could sense the adventure in her, the excitement, the sexuality, if you please. Of course these things do not matter to us, since we don't reproduce by such primitive means. To be strictly accurate, we don't reproduce at all. But her sexuality had a sort of static, it moved me tremendously. And so I slipped in, and we sat watching the Himalayas together, as the paint dried on her long nails, and the old clock, specially imported from England by the missionary Cockerell, struck the hour of six, the mellow chimes reverberating in this beautiful room, in the clear Himalayan air. A servant woman came in and lit the fire, but Dona Rosa and I did not so much as acknowledge her hunched up old body as she waddled in and out.

Flames of gold licked the dark smoky walls of the fireplace, and a soft hissing sound coursed through the room. The sound of the fire was visible to me as it described a tremulous circle around us, like an expanded ring of cigarette smoke. It was good to sit in the quiet bosom of this beautiful woman and watch the effulgent evening glow that was suspended over the snow mountains, while here in the house, before the order and warmth of our hearth, the flames shot through the patient pine-cones and settled into embers.

I have my own limitations. Whereas the future (viewed in a certain light) is like a quicksilver stream capable of being gauged and understood, or an incoming bus that can be caught or missed, the past remains a mystery, to be grasped only in the chambers of memory. I knew – I sensed – Dona Rosa to the depths of her being, but her history, the particular truth of her past, could only be understood and reconstructed from scattered thought-impulses and shards and splinters of memory.

I am not a patient ghost. (How I detest that word!) In our

world too, we have our shortcuts and ways around things, our fixers and facilitators. I decided to appeal to the most venerable of the wise ones, our black brethren, the crows. Crows have ancient eyes, they look into the twenty-seven depths of surface events and understand their totality. There is nothing they do not know. Their opinionated cousins, the ravens, are parvenus and pretenders, the object of much pity and ridicule in refined circles. The walrus, I understand, is acquainted with death, with the synapse between the worlds. The cat too is companion to many mysteries. But it is the crow, lustrous, black, benign in the indifference of its cold intellect, which can be trusted totally in delicate matters.

The Himalayan crow, in particular, is cognisant of the power of dreaming and receptive to the web of interconnectedness. I do not leave my habitation much, but my friends the crows are eternal wanderers. Much that I have learnt in the course of my existence has been gleaned from the feathered denizens of the deodar tree that fronts the house. (I have always, at a distance of course, admired the spirit of the deodar, a dryad of beauteous charm, courteous, gracious, a true *vanbhanjika*. I have not so far ventured her closer acquaintance, but it is a promise I have made to myself – only the moment is not yet ripe.)

There is a time, just before dawn, in the last throes of the night, when the crows talk. Their words and their visions are known to the wise as the *kagbhushandi*, the speech of crows. That night I left the comforting confines of Dona Rosa's bosom and visited my friends. They were waiting for me, alert and motionless, just the set and turn of a beak or the ruffling of a wing to indicate their seriousness. The lady of the deodar was asleep, or absent, yet I could sense her presence in the quiet majesty of her home. I could not but contrast the warm-blooded tumult of Dona Rosa's heart with the serene sanctuary of the admirable *vanbhanjika*.

I sat listening to my friend KailKaran, the most wise and learned among crows. In the language that came before words, he told me all he knew of Dona Rosa. I was not disappointed in her past. When the crows (three young and five old) flew towards the dawn with a white sheet woven of the woof and warp of potentiality and inevitability, the cloth held in between their black beaks, as they flew in stately procession and formal alignment, I pierced the membrane of things-gone-by and in a flash, as at the moment of drowning, Dona Rosa's life came to me.

There is a critical distinction between observing an object from a single direction and observing it from all possible directions simultaneously. Dona Rosa was born under the star of travel and change. Her earliest memory of herself was in a church – the Dom in Berlin, replete with cherubs and angels and gold, gold everywhere. Her mother's hand, soft as roses and yet hard as a vice, gripping her angrily by the wrist even as her face remained in its habitual set of piety and repose. Dona Rosa – but that is not her name then, she is just little Laura, Tatiana's daughter – little Laura wants urgently to pee, she has just told her mother that, but of course it is not to be, it would not be appropriate, in the midst of the chorale, as the mightiest organ in Europe transports everyone but Laura towards heavenly delights – how could Tatiana then trip over the pews to escort her daughter out?

She pinches Laura once again, there is a degree of malice in that pinch, and then suddenly the trumpets sound, they are urgent and insistent, as is the call of the little girl's bladder. Resignedly Laura looks up at the huge dome of the church, it is like being inside a perfectly shaped breast, and then suddenly, as her eyes reach the top of the dome, she sees it there, spreadeagled against the sky, its stained-glass wings beating with a passion she recognises. 'What is that?' she whispers in her mother's ear, holding her by the chin in the irritating way she has, guiding her vision up to where the sacred spirit beats against the walls and confines of the church.

Her mother, the noble and long-suffering Tatiana, looks up, and for a second her gaze is held by the sacredness of the vision and the fervour of the child beside her. Extraordinarily moved, she kisses the little girl, and in the honey-and-spice voice for which she is famous, tells Laura that it is none other than the Holy Ghost, the Spirit of God.

As I sat listening and learning from the crows, as the dryad of the deodar slept her enchanted sleep, as the world turned and the moon waned and as the distant light of the sun lit up the day, I saw Laura's grandmother, Tatiana's mother, mistress of fifty thousand serfs, even as she faced the ragged and hostile crowd in her estate outside Moscow, near the Sparrow Hills.

Another memory, which I picked from the core of Dona Rosa's self. It is a grainy memory, like an old photograph: she has forgotten it but it persists in the recesses of her mind, in her heart, it has touched her far more than she can imagine or recollect. It lives on in every cell in her body, this memory of her childhood, when she, my love Dona Rosa, is wearing a pretty dress, a flowered print, and her clear eyes and child's face are framed by cleverly cascading curls which her mother has carefully manipulated.

There is a fish bowl in the room; it is a dark gloomy room with the blinds shut and the curtains down, yet I know that there is blazing sun outside. In the fish bowl there is a dead fish, its body swollen, its eyes bulging with new and apocalyptic knowledge.

My little Laura (for she is not of course yet the Dona Rosa that I was to know) sees this fish, and she is moved by an immense sympathy and caritas. She wants to bring the fish back to life again, she wants to breathe her life breath into it. Very carefully she extracts it from the thick glass bowl, the bowl which has orange lines around the top and a gold line around its wobbling bottom. She lays the fish in the palm of her hand and seats herself on the edge of an enormous chair to contemplate the inert object. She knows the fish is dead, but she is a stubborn girl, she does not give up so easily. Nothing is irrevocable: everything must yield to change.

But nothing changes: the fish is still dead, it lies compliantly in the palm of her hand, awaiting re-life. Moved by some internal memory, Laura takes out an imaginary powder from the pocket of her flowered dress and sprinkles it over the cold orange blob. It moves – or perhaps it doesn't: but she is an optimist, and she takes it out, to the garden where a blinding sun is beating down on the lilypool where a fountain lies dry, to the lilypool where goldfish flash in the cool water. She throws the dead fish in – it leaps in, she is sure it leaps in – and she goes back to her play, satisfied with the day's work.

At this moment of my ramblings I am already in love with little Laura, for I can see her here before me, in the eager curiosity with which Dona Rosa accosts her world, in the unsettling challenge of her beauty. I can recognise her in the way Dona Rosa stares at the faraway snow peaks, in the studious serenity with which she brushes her hair.

I must explain how very difficult it is for us spirits to really see you humans. First of all there is the problem of perspective; then the distortion inherent in the process of conversion. In spite of all this, although her image was only a simulated, refracted version of her self-perception, Dona Rosa looked beautiful and beguiling and very womanly. I have a weakness for women, for the feminine principle really, it's nothing I'm ashamed of.

Words are clumsy and inadequate vehicles of my perception. They are globular, unidimensional, weighted with prejudice. The reasons for my choosing, or being chosen by, this channel are connected with the humans who have peopled this house, their auras sensing mine, our linkages, the joy of talking. When we see things in our dimension, we view them in so many ways that are completely unfamiliar to your way of seeing – in such a simultaneity and flux of perception – that perhaps after all it would be simpler to come and transport you to my world. But I am tired, dispirited, even a little bored, and I need to talk, especially about her.

I realised that very first day (for I had now entered the space of hours and days) that she knew about our world. Not that she was completely informed, but she had her suspicions and her intuitions. I could see it in her eyes, amber flecked with black, and in that disconcerting look, so direct and yet so deceptively helpless, with which she had turned to the man as he came in. The eyes are important, for the eyes are the highway to the soul. That is where we can be glimpsed, me and my kind, inhabitants of the shadows.

This man – ah, I'd better start telling the story better – this man was Captain Wolcott, a friend and student of the magician Aleister Crowley, the 'great beast' so reverenced by Munro and Marcus. Wolcott was a stupid, simpering sort of man with a body of anger inside him, and this anger gave him heat and sexuality and made him attractive to women. Dona Rosa had met him on the ship to India, on a moonlit night, on the decks of the P. & O. steamer where she sat watching for mermaids and falling stars. She had imagined that they fell in love, but of course it was nothing like that, it was just karma, and her destiny, which drew her as a string pulls a kite, to this house, high on the mountains, where I was waiting, bored, restless and uncertain.

I once knew, through interconnections, of a spirit who resided in a malicious parrot who had somehow got entangled with an amorous Lucknow courtesan. It was a complicated and confused matter – a cautionary tale for the disembodied. This spirit – it was habitually reckless – broke the cardinal rule. It forgot who it was. When I saw Dona Rosa, all the selves who stood before and after her, I realised that I was in mortal danger. I hesitated, I deliberated whether to turn back. Even now it was not too late. Back in the safety of my own dimension I could retreat to a world of grace and courtesy, and once again dream of the dryad in the deodar tree.

It is never good to venture too far, for mysteries are fragile things, and every world and dimension is full of traps for the unwary. I hesitated, and you could say that in that hesitation I was lost. You will understand what I mean; it happens often enough with your kind.

Dawn broke, and the mysteries of the night were dispelled. I scurried back to my spot behind the curtain, my special place, my safe place, the place where I belonged. The journey had sapped me, and I was anxious and enervated. I resolved to forget this folly, and I even considered leaving my spot and finding another place or dimension in which to await my moment of transition. But such things are not easy, they do not happen just like that, they have to be ordained. And of course I had made my choice, I had already embraced my destiny.

All day I tried to keep away from Dona Rosa. She had been busy writing letters, reading the tarot, examining her beautiful face in the tarnished mirror, smiling at herself, at the sunset. The laws of karma continue to confound me, despite the many magicians and philosophers I have trespassed. But, as Dona Rosa's hands faltered over the spread-out pack of tarot cards, I glimpsed for a moment the nature of human choice. Choice is the joker in life's pack of cards. It is choice that first guides the sperm on its long wet journey. Lonely, desirous of success, impelled by both past and future, it knows that its destiny is waiting, pulling it to the tip of the cape, the isthmus of the mother. Life is a constant series of choices. Some you make, and some are inevitably made for you.

Captain Wolcott strode in on his long, strong legs. The draughty fireplace, constructed by some inept hill man, was glowing with the stable heat of a stump of oak, carried painstakingly from the forest outside by one of the several rugged Pahari matrons who worked for the white men they called the sahib-log. It was a badly constructed fireplace, the proportions were wrong, yet it was the focus of the room, its centre, the natural point to which everyone gravitated. It is easy for our kind to see and understand fire. It is a helpmeet, an ally; once you know the nature of fire it is easy to handle and subdue. The trouble with fire is that it is friendly, it is gregarious, it reaches out without reservation. It does not have the discretion, the decorum, of water. Yet fire is a moody element, it can be playful one minute, vicious the next. You have to constantly humour it. It is one of the barriers. It does not acknowledge us, but we know how to ride the wind with it, how to play it.

Captain Wolcott was standing before the fire. He was lost in thought. His handsome, well proportioned face was perplexed. I could feel the flames warming his knees, the heat insinuating its way up his body. The bunion on the fourth toe of his left leg was acting up, and under the tightly laced shoes his socks smelt foul.

Dona Rosa came up to him and kissed him lightly on the cheek. No part of his anatomy responded to her; he was anxious and perplexed, staring at the fire with his mouth agape like the fool that hc was. I knew better than he did what was troubling him: his sister had sent him a letter, not yet delivered, in fact it was never to be delivered, informing him that his creditors were getting desperate. Besides, the local water had got to him, there were worms swimming like sharks in his intestines, eating up his sustenance. Dona Rosa gave him another languishing look, and yet another kiss.

I felt spiteful. The man was a fool, he didn't deserve that kiss. A spark, a tiny fraction of fire, jumped out of the heap of pine-cones scattered around the oak log. It defied gravity and embraced him exactly where Dona Rosa had planted her kiss. I had nothing to do with it, I can swear that; perhaps it was inadvertent. Control is never easy between dimensions.

Walter Wolcott let out a tiny yelp of pain, and Dona Rosa rushed to his side, the very picture of solicitude. She kissed him again, on the very same spot. Her naturally pink lips, on which she had put a salve of crushed rosebuds and honey, touched and embraced his. He responded to her this time; the fire had finally warmed him, he had forgotten about the creditors, he wanted to further forget about them.

One kiss led to another, and in a short while they were all tangled up in each other, the unsightly heap of holes and orifices and protruding parts which your race understands as passion. I was dismayed to see the change in Dona Rosa. The proud nobility, the gentle calm of her demeanour all vanished from view. She led Wolcott on as a jockey spurs a horse, an oarsman a boat, her amber eyes flashing with lust and greed and calculation.

Emotions almost always have markers. They are palpable, and

we find them easier to understand than, for instance, thoughts, which require a degree of indoctrination to penetrate. I was, frankly, surprised and a little dismayed by the intensity of Dona Rosa's ardour. Still I decided to transpose to the body of her partner, the well-built Captain Wolcott. Once within him, ensconced in the driver's seat, I experienced tremors of fear, and a mind so vacuous and malleable that I found myself in control from the very start. I cannot say that this was good, for there was no challenge in it.

A man's body is a most peculiar construct. A woman's body contains a symmetry of purpose – the breasts, which are the conduit of the life-force, and the womb, the matrix of life. A man is an idiot on two legs, with a tap of semen between the testicles: his life-force is stored in a vulnerable exterior container. I was not enamoured of Wolcott's body, and in particular I found his organ, engorged with blood and lust, a most inadequate vehicle to reach and penetrate the essence of my beloved Dona Rosa. The whole process was senseless. Yet I was possessed, I could not withdraw from my need of her to the more abstract and exalted joys of my own domain.

Dona Rosa sensed the change, and her eyes lit up with interest and speculation. In my many years of solitude, this was the first time I had succumbed to lust. We rode each other for many hours, thrusting and seeking, withholding and giving. The oak log burnt on brightly through the night. The Pahari women-servants from the outhouses peeped in, dinner trays balanced on their chafed, knobbly hands. They peered in through the curtains, for Dona Rosa had not seen fit to lock the door, and nodding sagely retreated into the servants' quarters and puffed quietly at their cheroots, sometimes breaking the silence to hum an old folk song. They had seen worse.

We made love deep into the night, exchanging kisses and snorts and moments of deep quietude. One of the windows was still open, and the mountain breeze poured into the room. I was enchanted by the consistency of her flesh, its soft feel, its creamy texture, its corporeality. Deep between her thighs lay an abyss of detachment, an island of certainty. It was here that life swam to refashion itself; it was here that the mysteries of creation swarmed. Here was the secret I longed to penetrate, the sanctuary in a sacred womb until I was refashioned and reborn.

I still remember what it was like in there, dark and warm, pulsating with joyous movement, utterly secure and yet containing the abandonment of imminent destruction. Of course, it was claustrophobic in a way – and then there was Wolcott's sperm, a sticky river of life and death, of triumph and abject defeat. In the end it was a relief to get out, to return to the open spaces.

Wolcott served me well; nature had endowed him generously and his limbs had grace and vigour. His mind, however, was flaccid and full of the most horrid pretensions. As he sat astride my beloved his head flickered with a load of book-read rubbish; he thought of Lilith, and the sisters of Satan, and other such emblems of easy perversion. His mind was so crowded with purchased images that he could not see the priceless treasure that he had before him, Laura in the haystack, in the autumn sun, as the farmhand touched her with his tender fingers which knew how to make things grow.

I realised that she had picked up my perception. She looked at me with mild surprise. It was the first time that we had talked. Communication is rare between species: between dimensions it is even more precious.

Later, our passion relenting, we left the room and sat in the balcony, watching the stars. Orion was spread across the sky, the wind wept in the soft tresses of the deodar tree, and Sirius, the dog star, glittered like a madman's eye in the inky Himalayan night.

'*The Pleiades have fled, and I am here alone,*' she told Wolcott. 'That's from Sappho.'

'Crowley was the greatest poet of the century,' Wolcott responded, 'greater even than that posturer Yeats!' He cleared his throat and began humming in a deep clear voice that cut through the night air like a sword –

> '*Io Pan! Io Pan!*
> *Io Pan! Io Pan! Come over the sea*
> *From Sicily and from Arcady!*
> *Roaming as Bacchus, with fauns and pards,*
> *And nymphs and satyr for thy guards,*
> *On a milk-white ass, come over the sea*
> *To me, to me.*'

'That was by Crowley,' he said. 'I've heard it sung during the mysteries at his house in Boleskine. I've always wondered, darling – do you see me as Apollo or Dionysus? Could one be a bit of both?'

My beloved gave him a look of such withering contempt that a more sensitive human might have cringed: but Wolcott, oblivious to all, squeezed her hand ardently and began humming the same tune again.

Meanwhile a swarm of fireflies wafted past us in the forest below. Dona Rosa clapped her hands in childish delight. 'How utterly delightful!' she murmured excitedly. 'How I wish they would come up to meet me!'

Her wish was my command. Subsuming myself in their energies, I led them up to the balcony to pay homage to her beauty. The docile creatures danced around her like stars, and then I bade them go, for excessive beauty is unbearable to the inner logic of life. It breeds death and despair and deep discontent. Even in my besotted state I had not forgotten that. Have you seen a firefly in the morning? Before the light of the day it is a shrivelled, naked insect, a forlorn grub. So, Father Benedictus had told me, in the course of our long conversations, when he came to exorcise the house of Munro and his metaphysical games, so does temporal human love pale before the eternal love of God.

Our kind is not nourished by the sun: it is the moon which gives us sustenance. We wax and wane with the moon, except when harnessed by a human energy, when the pull of the tides loses its grip. As dawn broke over the mountains, lighting up the still white presence of the snows, first to an unearthly grey, and then a flushed radiant pink, I too fled to my refuge, my fated spot. This night of passion, my first, had initiated me into the sorrows of mankind, the unfaith, the terrible and tenuous link of love.

Impelled by a fatal curiosity, I delved into Wolcott. It was truly a distasteful job. Low-frequency beings leave a void in their wake, and Wolcott's confused, mendacious psyche created a degree of resistance that sapped me until I was actually tired. Walter Wolcott had no core, no centre, no focus, no definition. Greed, prejudice and overreaching clashed and combined with random force in his mind. He was an adventurer, a gambler, constantly cowering under the consequences of his own stupidities. Yet he considered himself a magician, a Master of the Universe.

Captain Wolcott had published a slim volume of poetry, after the Greek style, when he was eighteen. It had been plagiarised from his sister and was well received. He had never been in the army, of course. That went without saying. I wondered why he had remained a captain. Perhaps it was only a question of credibility and discretion – with the passage of years we would find him a general. I knew of course that this was not to be, that the passage of years was not for him. He had not then the odour of death, which is an odour that attaches itself to humans some six to eight months prior to their departure. He smelt still of pines and fine cigars and cologne water.

He had an impoverished, malignant mind, of the sort that rails against its own lack of resources and then resorts to sensation-seeking for gratification. Magic is, as you doubtless know, merely a matter of finding and making the right connections. I have seen men drink blood from bowls of bleached skulls: such revels were not unknown in the history of this very house, when mad Munro and his friend Marcus tried their metaphysical tricks in this same room so many years ago. I have seen these men burp and benefit nothing beyond. And then, I have seen wise men that but smile at the wind and have their way with the elements.

It was his looks that had led Dona Rosa to love him; that and her destiny. He was vain about his looks, and wore curlers in the bath. Laura, Dona Rosa, was, in the way of beautiful women, not very wise: she did not even know about the curlers. Any ordinary wife or trollop would have snooped through his possessions, seen the love letters from his abandoned wife, the woollen socks knitted by his sister, the admonishing note from his mother which the fool Wolcott carried with him in his baggage across the continents. But then Dona Rosa was, by her own estimation, clairvoyant.

Why had Wolcott made this journey to the East? He had travelled to Ceylon, where he first encountered his mentor, Aleister Crowley. The great Beast, the Master Thereon, 666, in the world of men upon the earth, Aleister Crowley of Trinity College, Cambridge, had taken pity upon him and adopted him as a pet. Awed by the palpable aura and power of that remarkable personage, he had hung on to Crowley like a stray pup. After the publication of his first and only book of poetry, written by his sister, financed by his mother, Wolcott had become a member of the Order of the Golden Dawn, and plunged into the study of the magical books of Wronski and Eliphaz Levi with fledgling enthusiasm. He read the poetry of Ernest Dowson and Oscar Wilde. He despised Yeats, and was convinced that his friend Crowley was a greater poet than the Irishman.

This man Aleister Crowley had entered my consciousness before. I had heard Munro and Marcus chatter about him as they went about their juvenile rites. Crowley had never come to our hills, but his spirit had traversed here to this far spot. It resided in this house, in the lost souls who travelled here, in the books he had written and, many years later, in the printed sleeve of a record album. It was on the cover of "Sergeant Pepper's Lonely Hearts Club Band", carried here by a group of trespassing young treckers, that I first saw Crowley's external manifestation – bald, kindly, a trifle amused.

It was in the music that I finally found him, so many years later, when the young woman who came in search of herself listened through the nights to the clanging atonal music of the Doors. I understood the man Crowley's insidious power to undo the work of civilisation, to unlock all that humans had for centuries tried to lock.

Wolcott had accompanied this same Crowley on a mountaineering expedition to Nepal. One afternoon, Wolcott and

Crowley were sitting in Crowley's tent, sipping tea. A Sherpa rushed in, panic in his voice as he reported an accident. A Swiss member of the team had been killed, and de Righi, an Italian hotel-keeper from Darjeeling, and three porters were still buried in the snow. Another Swiss member was missing.

Crowley looked up, amused, interested, stimulated. He liked death, especially other people's. 'I am sure that the good Swiss is old enough to rescue himself,' he intoned, in his jovial, fruity, faintly squeaky voice. 'As for de Righi, nobody could possibly want to rescue him.' Wolcott tittered unsurely, hero worship writ upon his handsome face. The Sherpa looked puzzled. Crowley was getting into form.

'My dear boy, a mountain accident of this sort is one of the things for which I have no sympathy whatsoever. Tomorrow I hope to go down and find how things stand.' He winked gaily at Wolcott as the Sherpa stared on uncomprehendingly. The three Sherpa lives were not of course at a premium in any calculation. As Crowley later explained to Wolcott, 'Porters aren't people!' Such is the nature of evil. It is, like Crowley and Wolcott, trivial and stupid and entirely sure of itself.

Crowley of course does not agree. He reaches across time and space and dimension, in what he would term his astral body, to educate me. He informs me, a little superciliously, that in the magical doctrine there are several levels of evil, some of which, paradoxically, belong to dimensions of equilibrium.

The first is the resistance of form to force, the evil of inertia. This is no true evil, but a function of equilibrium and process. The second level lies in Chaos, the Cosmic Quicksands. This evil, the evil of Old Night, the fear of the dark, evolves from lack of resistance. The third form of evil is the evil of imbalance, of unbalanced, displaced forces. So Crowley tells me, now that the story is over.

I myself am, in truth, nothing but a displaced force, yet I deny that I am evil. Perhaps indeed there is no evil. This man Crowley uses far too many words. But when he and Wolcott drank tea and watched the Himalayan sunset and mocked the dying, I feel that what they did was not good.

It is the spirits of the three Sherpas that were hounding Wolcott still. They are a bloodthirsty race, and vengeance is their creed. They stalked him, impatiently awaiting the moment of retribution, which would also be their moment of release. Crowley had already been dealt with.

Wolcott had lived briefly with Crowley in Paris. He was evicted from a series of hotels when he and 'the Beast' had refrained from paying their bills. Money, in my observations, has all the symptoms of magic, yet this simple-minded man resisted all his life from attaining its sympathetic pleasure, and pined instead for the obscure joys of telekinesis and mind-reading and the material mutations of the magical creed.

Crowley had cast Wolcott's horoscope and made a believer out of him. He found great reassurance in the cosmos, in astrology, numerology and the occult. It satisfied his inner need for unity and order, the same need army life had once fulfilled.

He studied the cabbala, and astral charts, and the Tree of Life, with earnest endeavour but to no avail. Meanwhile, he signed a cheque at Crowley's behest and thought that magic could shield him from the consequences. And so, to avoid unpleasantness, he became Captain Wolcott and made his way to India, to our remote mountains, where he nestled safe in the breast of Dona Rosa, that queen of dissimulators.

Laura, who by then had become Dona Rosa for reasons far too private to share with you, was on the fishing fleet to India. They fell in love in a welter of confused identities and mixed emotions. Dona Rosa had a fatal combination of beauty and forgiveness: men were quick to recognise and exploit this. A friend of Wolcott's had written to him about a house in the Himalayan mountains, outside an army cantonment near Almora, which was available for a song. The house stood in thirteen acres of orchard and garden, and was staffed by an ample number of willing native familiars. Moreover, it had been 'used for Magical and Mystical purposes' by mad Munro, a student and disciple of the occult, and his friend Marcus.

I take leave of you here to divert the course of my tale, and recount briefly the previous history of the house. While Wolcott sleeps soundly after his night of passion, I shall inform you about my encounters with those two charlatans, those pathetic impostors who polluted this house and its environs with their stupidities.

Both Munro and Marcus were silly dilettantes with an appetite for pain and sadism. Munro fancied himself as a hunter, and every weekend he and his cronies would get the locals to scour the surrounding forests of oak and deodar for young panthers, which they caught in cleverly laid traps and brought to the big house. These maimed animals, their spirits wounded and angry, would be taken to the tennis court, which was a few steps below the garden that fronted the house. There, they would be tied with long ropes to special posts erected for that very purpose. For one week they would undergo a special regimen, some of them extravagantly fed with veal and viands, some starved until they grew weak with hunger.

Captivity is anathema to the spirit of the panther: its essence is speed and agility and freedom. Animal energies, when released, remain in the air for a long time, and a permanent miasma of anger, sorrow and confusion had settled on the tennis court. Even the servants were reluctant to go there, and their recalcitrance was prodded with bribes and threats. Once, Munro even pushed a hill man into the pit of hungered beasts, but he escaped and ran away from the house, never to return. He would be haunted to the end of his days by the stench of confined animals and the sixty slits of green fire that stared at him through the dark night as, saved by a talisman his mother had given him, he ran for his life.

The panther is a black animal, and anger, when sheathed in the colour black, magnifies and multiplies and attains an unimaginable intensity until it implodes. Because of its feline nature the panther is able to impregnate many dimensions. In short, it is dangerous in the extreme. Yet these mavericks, these masqueraders posing as magicians, played with these mighty forces with the impunity of fools. It will not surprise you that they had to reap the consequences.

On moonless nights, always on moonless nights, the tennis court would be lit up with burning torches of cactus bush. Munro and Marcus and their friends, a mixed lot of vagrants and vagabonds that included a deposed Indian prince, a defrocked priest and the wife of an English colonel, would carouse and revel through the night. They would drink the blood of slaughtered goats, from the skull that sat on Munro's desk, from silver goblets, from an ever-diminishing stock of crystal wineglasses, and sometimes from the slippers of the Colonel's lady.

There would be a lot of talk, as I understand there always is at dinner parties. They would debate the role of improvisation in magical ritual, and take sides about the efficacy of Hindu tantric practices in Occidental garb. The Colonel's wife – Rita, that was her name – invariably got involved in arcane discussions about what the blood they were drinking really symbolised.

'It's just like in the church, really,' she would say, her narrow eyebrows raised in nervous concentration, 'except of course this is not the blood of Christ.'

The priest, the disgraced, defrocked priest, loved this kind of talk. 'Precisely, my dear lady! That is what the Eucharist proclaims – *Hoc est enim Corpus meum* – "This is my Body". And even St Paul has said "Without the shedding of blood there is no remission." Who are we to dispute St Paul?' he would exclaim, with pulpit authority.

They were, all in all, an earnest lot of people, but their collective aura was ugly in the extreme. For some, magic was a release from the tedium of daily life, for others, a means of seizing power, a form of conditioned greed, a result of the accretions of privilege by which their imbalanced souls were weighted.

Sometime around midnight mad Marcus would stagger through the room, urging his guests to silence. He would clamber atop one of the chairs before the fireplace and address his friends. His short speech, as I remember it, usually went something like this: 'My noble brethren! Let us remember today the ways of the ancient Magicians. Every living being is a storehouse of energy, varying in quantity according to the size and health of the animal, and in quality according to its mental and moral character. At the death of the animal, this energy is suddenly liberated.'

Once, at this stage of his oration, he fell off the chair and had to be propped up again, the Colonel's wife, Rita, holding him up with her gloved hands on the one side, the Indian prince on the other.

'The only sacrifice pleasing to the guardian spirits of the Universe, to the deliverers of all Life, is the sacrifice of Blood. Never forget, the Blood is the Life! Come, dear friends, let us feast on the energies of the Universe, let us become Immortal!'

Upon this signal the entire group of friends would rush to the balcony, where the servants were stationed in waiting with the weapons, and open fire upon the helpless panthers. The smell of cordite and the smell of blood would soak and seep through the night, corrupting the pure Himalayan air, and the carnage would only increase their appetite for dissipation.

Our kind do not possess blood, neither do we possess life. Their thirsts were incomprehensible to me, and I longed to rush to the aid of the massacred animals, to ease them in their passage. But it was not in my power, it was outside my strength. I could only watch as the band of brave seekers would invoke Abel and Cain, and Haman and Mordecai, and chatter on about Beelzebub and the Behemoth, for it is easy enough to feel courageous with a gun. Yet even in the midst of the slaughter the guardian spirits of the panthers were silent and watching.

Magic is interventionist, it is about gratification, instant gratification. It does not allow the forces of the universe to play themselves out. Father Benedictus explained this to me much later, when we were puzzling over the trail of pain that lay behind us. In their case, the foolish fiddling with the momentum and equilibrium of life-forces was to set into motion a chain of consequences that did not spare even the gentle spirit of the dryad of the deodar tree.

'Love is the law,' Marcus told Munro tenderly, as, satiated with their play, they left for their bedroom, a cloud of hemp and heroin trailing after them. The sacred hemp, the *bhang* of the hills, grew in wild abundance over the estate. Not content with nature's bounty, the hill men ritually cultivated the cannabis, planting it only at an ordained hour of a moonless Amavasya night. Marcus and Munro and their set were habituated to this weed, which gave them a tremendous appetite, both physical and sexual, and made them easier for the servants to handle. Added to this was the devious bliss of heroin, which the deposed prince, an enormous, grisly presence, had introduced them to. Human minds are intrinsically weak unless they are kept in careful check by the physical counter-motion of their bodies. The servants at the house were little better than indolent slaves, and pandered to every perverted whim and wish of their demonic masters with a fatalistic resignation. Lazy to the bone, rotten to the core, far from home and the censure of their peers, the two friends succumbed to their new pleasure.

The search for freedom that had initiated them into the occult had already degenerated into an escape from boredom. Their Anglo-Saxon upbringing did not give them the strength to sustain the guilt and inner tensions of their condition. There are, I understand, many racial types, not so alienated from the earth and the sky, who can easily internalise these polarities. However, Marcus, whose family knew him only as Mark, and Munro the Mad were not seers or mystics. The hashish, the heroin, the boredom, the freedom, caused a final rift between internal and external perceptions. In short, they went mad, raving mad.

Their jaded sexual appetites, constantly starving for fresh stimulus, now led them to new and desperate depravities. Virgins were brought in, dozens of them, and since in these hills among certain of their tribes, a Nayak marriage can be contracted for the payment of a bride-price, it was easy to keep them in good supply. But the sturdy hill women, though supple and beauteous in their youth, lacked the maidenly refinement that was such an important concomitant of their ravishment. Besides, Marcus complained that they smelt intolerable, they smelt of cows and sweat, and it had become a chore to work his way through them. An increasingly difficult chore, for every appetite must perforce flag, and so when the Staff of Life failed to rise to their calls, when the Elixir of Eternity stopped flowing from their bodies, when impotent middle age impeded their great Quest, fear and panic set in: panic about life, fear of death.

In the manner of academics, with the earnestness of initiates, with the touching faith of fools, they consulted their books. 'Every man has the right to fulfil himself to the utmost,' Marcus told Munro, in the motherly tone of a woman telling a bedtime tale. 'Every man has the right to fulfil his own will without being afraid that it may interfere with that of others; for if he is in his proper place, it is the fault of others if they interfere with him.' Rumpling his lover's hair, he examined him tenderly. 'Hmm, that's pretty clear. I'd say we are in our proper places, aren't we?'

It was decided by the little band of initiates that the best course to revive their flagging energies would be to throw a virgin to the black beasts of the night. As the priest explained, 'All corpses are sacred unto me; they shall not be touched save in mine Eucharist. That, dear brothers, is what the Book commands. That is what needs to be done.'

The Colonel's lady looked up from her copy of the Book. 'A virgin is what is important,' she said, her narrow eyebrows furrowed in excitement, a sweep of lust convulsing her body. 'A virgin has not lost her potential energy, she has not been diminished! We need a virgin!'

Marcus looked up, an expression of distaste flooding his handsome face. His long hair shone like a golden mane in the firelight. 'I've had enough of virgins!' he exclaimed. 'I think their purity is highly overrated. The only ones available have filthy minds and filthier bodies – they are not vestal enough. What we need is male energy – a reservoir of uncorrupted primordial masculine energy.'

This was precisely the sort of abstract theological talk the disgraced priest loved. Eagerly he turned to the Book. 'Yes!' he responded enthusiastically. 'That's exactly what it says here . . . I've located the precise passage that confirms your intuitions.' Clearing his throat he read it aloud in a theatrical, somewhat self-conscious voice, his spectacles making him look almost benign.

'"For the highest spiritual working one must accordingly choose that offering which contains the greatest and purest force. A male child of perfect innocence and high intelligence is the most satisfactory and suitable offering."'

There was a moment of silence as the group contemplated this. He cleared his throat yet again. 'For evocations it may be more convenient to place the blood of the victim in the Triangle – the idea being that the spirit obtains from this blood the subtle but physical substance which is the quintessence of its life, in such a manner as to enable it to take on a visible and tangible shape.' Munro sneezed, a loud, violent sneeze that startled everybody.

The priest continued, undeterred: '"This Bloody sacrifice is the critical point of the World Ceremony of the Proclamation of Horus, the Crowned and Conquering Child, as Lord of the Aeon."' Munro sneezed again; he was developing a cold.

'So it is prophesied, and so it shall be,' the priest concluded, a little lamely.

Rita was staring at him in horror. 'A child?' she exclaimed, her eyes clouding over, her narrow brows peaking like mountains. 'Are you suggesting that we should kill a child? A poor, innocent child? But that's barbaric.'

'My dear lady, that is the mother in you responding,' the deposed Indian prince said gently. His voice and accent were different from those of the others, and although he was gross and fat, he looked oddly compassionate, even sorrowful. He and the Colonel's lady were lovers. They had at that moment little hatred in them.

Mad Munro came centre-stage. As was his habit, he clambered up the wooden chair that stood before the fireplace and held up his hand for silence. His shadow wavered on the wall behind him, and he looked oddly impressive, like a Roman senator or pedagogue. '"Until the Great Work has been performed, it is presumptuous for the Magician to pretend to understand the Universe, and dictate its policy,"' he said, reading out from the book he held in his hand. The room was dark and full of shadows, and I wondered how his human eyes could read in that dim light.

'Slay that innocent child?' I hear the ignorant say. 'What a horror!' 'Ah!' replies the Knower, with the foresight of history, 'but that child will become a Nero! Hasten to strangle him!'

He sneezed again, and blew his nose with a crumpled checked handkerchief which he extracted from the depths of his trouser pocket. He pointed his finger, the handkerchief still in his hand, at the little assembly. His eyes were bloodshot and his voice was echoing through the room like thunder. 'And there is a third, above these, above all these, who understands that Nero was as necessary as Julius Caesar.'

*

I was getting tired of human talk, it used too many words, and their hysteria sickened me. I reverted to another dimension, a dimension of peace, such immense empty solitude that sometimes it is difficult to penetrate. But at that moment it was just what I needed and I made it there, somehow. In the bright light of my world I wondered about my own past.

I do not remember who I was, in the other life, or if I was ever there at all. Individual memories are the memories of humans. When they die, their psychic residues spill over to our world, to other worlds. Their collapsing energies emanate a mighty helplessness, clogging up consciousness, making it difficult to comprehend or switch over to other spheres. I knew at that moment that someone had died.

When I returned to my spot behind the curtain, the child was already dead. It lay before the fireplace. A circle of chalk was drawn around it, and a thin trickle of blood flowed out of the circle on to the polished wooden boards.

The infant's eyes were open; large sentient eyes that were staring at the ceiling or something beyond. His lips were spread in a sad smile. Marcus felt a stab of some emotion he could not identify. He bent down and wiped a blotch of blood from the child's abdomen, then wondered what to do with the handkerchief.

I could sense that the infant had already forgiven them. This was an evolved soul, wandering through time, born only to cause hurt and pain to its mother and light the fire of unforgiving revenge in its Rajput father, and to set in a motion an incomprehensible karmic cycle that would destroy everything that I loved in its wake. But the child itself left behind no anger, no fear, no emanations. An unsettling quiet pervaded the room.

Now that a male infant had been slaughtered, now that they had participated in the mystery of its flesh, nobody seemed to know quite what to do with it. They consulted their usual sources, but the Book said nothing. The servant who had been bribed to steal the child from his mother had already fled home to his village, sixty miles away from the house. Marcus suggested that they chuck it into the fireplace, but that was clearly not a good idea. Rita was of the opinion that they bring it back to life. 'There are passages in the Book that suggest it can be done,' she said tremulously. 'And besides, we have the example of the Resurrection.' The men looked at her contemptuously and said nothing. The killing had made them hungry. The Prince wrapped up the baby in old newspapers, newspapers that had come all the way from England, and placed it in the bottom drawer of Munro's desk. It had hardly bled at all. Then he put his arms around Rita and led her gently out of the room.

The next great panther hunt was approaching, and several young animals had been caught in anticipation of the event. They were, as usual, tied on long ropes to the stumps on the tennis court. After dinner, which was served in the dining room downstairs (roast lamb, mint sauce, cutlets, potatoes, steamed ginger pudding, prepared by a blind, drunken cook who was always complaining), Marcus went up to the study again. Staying clear of the chalk circle, he sat before the fire and lit himself a cigarillo. He studied the flames for a long time, thinking of nothing. You could say that he was pensive, even sad. The sadness of the child, its purity, had touched him somewhere. After he was through with his smoke he opened the bottom drawer of the desk, carried the packet out, and hurled the infant to the hungry animals.

*

In its home in Ranikhet, in the wooden house near the bazaar, with its carved rafters and warm kitchen smells, the child's mother was frantic with worry and grief. He was her firstborn, her most precious creature, and she had been nursing him still. Her milk overflowed from her full breasts and drenched her blouse even as her eyes filled with the tears she tried so hard to hold back. Her husband looked at her helplessly. He loved his young wife with a passion rare to husbands in these hills, and he could not bear to see her cry. He did not care about his son so much, even though it was a male and his firstborn. In fact he harboured a sense of active jealousy towards the love which was diverted to it. But he could not bear to see his wife weep.

He went to the sacred altar of the *ishta-devatas*, the household gods, and took out a silver bowl of vermilion powder. Carefully, ritually, he smeared a blood-red streak of vermilion across his noble Rajput forehead. 'I swear to you, Saruli,' he said to his wife, 'I will not step into this house again unless I have our child in my arms.'

Saruli's husband went from his home to the temple, not the Lakshmi Vishnu temple near his home and the bazaar, but to the bleak Bhairav temple that sat on a ridge where the forest pines whispered and birch and oak guarded the fierce secrets of the temple sanctuary. Here, in a ritual circle of stone and brick, a fire of wood and coal always smouldered. A tin kettle boiled upon a tripod placed among the ashes. Acts of unmentionable cruelty, acts of immense purity: the circle had witnessed them all. A few steps away, in a little shelter to the north, stood a small stone statue; more an obelisk than a statue, rather like the rough rectangular grinding-stones the hill women use for their spices.

Here in this stone, Maha-Kali was immanent, Maha-Kali the mistress of time; Shamshan-Kali, the deity of the cremation grounds; the primal strength of the mountains, the spirit of these hills.

The gods have always confused me, for their worlds have nothing to do with ours. Yet it is an important insight into the tangled skeins of time, into the playful web of unfolding, to observe that while Wolcott, who you the reader have all but forgotten, Wolcott and his hero Crowley, that vain, ill-educated autodidact, had sipped their gently brewed Darjeeling tea, which never tasted right in those high altitudes, in the shadow of the Kanchenjunga, it was this same Makalu, this same Maha-Kali, the spirit of Time, that the Sherpas had invoked as they lay dying in the cold snow, and the Englishmen sneered at their pain.

An old woman in ragged black clothes hobbled towards Saruli's husband. She dragged her right foot as though it were a great weight, and a grimace of pain sat permanently upon her simian features. Wordlessly she offered him some tea, strong, sweet tea in a brass cup without a handle. A mild drizzle was playing upon the ashes of the sacred circle, and the burning coals were hissing in protest at the water's transgressions. Several long swords, ceremonial swords with death-sharp blades spattered with the ritual blood of sacrifice, stood in a tall bin beside the oak tree that sheltered the main temple. Both of them, the old woman and the young man, were silent for a long time. Quietly they listened to the mountain breeze and to the contented cawing of crows, to the creeping fog, to the rain, to the fire. The vermilion tikka on the forehead of the child's father was wet, it was running down his nose, down his cheeks. When he wiped it off it was his hands that were stained with red.

She contemplated him sorrowfully, 'He is gone, chela,' she said, in a hoarse whisper that grated the very air. 'You are not destined to see him again.'

The chain of events which followed went something like this. The other lives, the lives of the servants who lived in the outhouses, those shadows I rarely encountered from my perch behind the curtain, their busy tumultuous lives which have nothing to do with our story, came into play. They collided for a while with the exalted presences of the white sahibs, the two stories got briefly and temporarily mixed up. A washerwoman who lived high in the hills above the house, who washed and ironed the clothes of the *sahib-log*, Munro's shirts, Marcus's underwear, who cleaned their dirt and uncreased their garments, this washerwoman became amorously entangled with a son of the village headman. He was a cheerful gallant boy, and he bought his beloved a pair of silver ear-rings, that and a silver ring, from the fair in Bageshwar.

That pleased her, it made her happy, and she yielded him her many treasures. But when she talked of marriage the sepoy could think only of his father, the village headman, that fierce upholder of dharma, to whom nothing in the world was as abhorrent as the intermingling of the castes, the confusion of bloodlines. The two met as usual at their normal trysting-place, a glade beside the forbidden tennis court where not even the most foolhardy ventured. Torn between his longing and his terror, the sepoy watched helplessly as the washerwoman threw her new silver earrings, and her ring, into the pit where the hungry panthers roamed, restrained by long ropes and the warped wills of the white men.

The washerwoman returned to her washing, her tight behind wiggling with venom at man's perfidy. The sepoy watched her departure with a mixture of lust and resignation, and then with a philosophical shrug he ventured valiantly into the tennis court, where, keeping clear of the angered panthers, whose combined fury was play compared to what he had just encountered, he began hunting for the silver earrings. At the edge of the field, where nettles and dandelion grew, the sepoy found the index finger of the slaughtered infant, a pathetic dried-up protuberance that had once clasped its mother's hand in trust. He knew, as every villager did, of Saruli's child that was lost, and her husband's vow not to return home until he found him. Forgetting for the moment about the silver earrings, and the washerwoman for whom he had got them, he rushed home to his father the village headman, or *mukhiya*, to inform him of his discovery.

The five elders of the village met at a formal *panchayat* to discuss what was to be done. 'We have been indulging these madmen too long,' the village headman said solemnly, his bushy moustache bristling with portent. 'It is time to retrieve our Pahari honour and show them that we are not afraid.'

They told Saruli's husband of what they had found, and although he was sorrowful he was resigned to his fate. With great stealth and secrecy the villagers collected panthers from forests far and near, and kept them in specially constructed wooden cages near the temple of Kalika in the ridge, where the crows meditate on the Goddess of Death and drink the blood from her sacrifices.

The cooks at the house began putting quantities of laxatives into the food. Marcus and Munro both began to have trouble with their insides, and in a week they were debilitated beyond belief. The great hunt was postponed, and the servants were instructed to feed the panthers to keep them in sustenance until the next moonless night.

On the Amavasya night, during the festival of Diwali, the festival of lights, the village headman came to visit Munro and his lover Marcus. He brought with him a hamper of sweets, and some fire-crackers, which were expensive and hard to come by in our villages in those days. Marcus and Munro, who had been reading the tarot in between their visits to the thunderbox, were gratified by this show of affection, in token of which they gave the village *mukhiya* a bottle of rum, and one of port as well for good measure. Although he was an abstemious man, the headman's expression as he accepted these gifts was sage, even benign.

In the midst of these smiling pleasantries, upon a prearranged signal the villagers, for once united, despite the boundaries of caste, by their common anger, let loose two score panthers they had brought with them, and beat them with drums and cries into the big house. Then, after securely locking the front door, they lit the firecrackers and celebrated the justice of their cause with the rum and the port.

Marcus and Munro, who had the luck of the Devil with them, ran up the stairs and managed to find refuge in the dressing room that connected the two bedrooms. They did not on their way there escape the attentions of the enraged beasts, Marcus lost an arm and Munro was mauled in the face. Although blood is repugnant to me, I was watching, watching and waiting, throughout the sorry spectacle, although I did not in any way intervene.

The entire house echoed with the soft padding of the panthers, the swishing of their enraged tails, the sighs and snarls with which they sought out their tormentors. They could smell the rancid fear emanating from the dressing room, and the spirits of their race awaited the equilibrium of revenge.

Munro reached out for his pistol, a handy Mauser which he kept hidden with his underwear in a drawer in the dressing room. When I saw the pistol in his hand, when I saw the inequity of that weapon, the relief and the empowerment which it conferred, a sense of distaste rose within me. Although I had nothing to do with it, a frightened hill monkey, a black and white langur cowering in the upper branches of the deodar tree, fainted and fell off its green arms in a fit of acute terror. The smells and sounds of the snarling panthers had reached him in his high shelter and, as is the way with hill monkeys, he swooned and fell. I do not think I was involved in any way, at least not voluntarily. Sometimes our impulses achieve a life of their own.

As the langur hurtled down to descend upon the slate roof of the house, the sound of his fall so startled the already terrified Munro that his pistol went off, the bullet searing though the heart of his paramour Marcus. As he lay dead in the dressing room, covered by the heat and power of his pouring blood, his beautiful face wore an expression of mild astonishment, the blue eyes surprised by the strange visions that confronted him as he made the transition from this world to the next.

Even mad Munro had feelings: he could not bear to be the instrument of his beloved Marcus's death, and he promptly shot himself in the temple in an excess of grief. I meant no mischief, the act and the incitement was theirs alone. And so these sorry journeyers to the East came to an ugly end, their delusions of omnipotence over a willing universe destroyed by stupidity and boredom.

The next day the panthers were fed with poisoned bait that was thrown into the house by the villagers. After the bodies of the dead animals had been disposed of, Saruli's husband entered the house, accompanied by the headman. It was deep into the dark night, and although the silence was oppressive, there was a calm about the rooms that convinced them that the Englishmen were indeed dead. They did not stay for long, for Paharis are superstitious and afraid of ghosts. The child's father looked around him, at the fluttering curtains, the brass beds, the counterpanes, the comfortable armchairs, the skull upon the desk. The tarot cards that the two had been reading, just before the *mukhiya* came to meet them, lay spread upon the desk. They saw the Hanged Man, with his contented fool's grin, and the reversed image of Death, the busy skeleton with its scythe, and the moon, La Lune, they saw these playthings on the Englishmen's table and averted their eyes from them, for these sights were not auspicious.

Although Saruli's husband was tough and wiry, a man who had once been in single combat with a marauding tiger and made good his escape, his stance and gait was that of a defeated man. He had retrieved his Thakur honour, the badge and pride of his caste, he had obtained his revenge, but he could never go back home again to his house near the bazaar. He had sworn to his wife that he would return with the child in his arms, and a Thakur does not break his word lightly.

As for the washerwoman, she whose silver earrings had wrought this revenge, she left the hills and became a successful courtesan of Bareilly.

It was only several days later that the officers at the army cantonment at Raneekhet came to hear rumours of the massacre. When they questioned the locals they met with a wall of silence. Marcus and Munro enjoyed an unsavoury reputation in the cantonment, but since they kept to themselves and caused no scandal they were let be. Now the solidarity of race and colour asserted itself, and the officers came to the big house in search of the two Englishmen.

It was a particularly fine day, with the sky the clear blue colour of late November. The snow mountains sat still and unmoving, every contour of their mighty massifs exposed in the pure winter air. The marigolds that flourish in the season flooded the gardens with their mellow fragrance. The last of the roses were still in bloom. Two huge rosebushes, one bearing white flowers, the other red, fronted the house. Yellow butterflies flitted about these bushes, feasting on the pollen, and where the overblown roses had fallen to the ground, fat grubs hid under their tender petals. A Himalayan bird of paradise swooped across the pathway, its golden crest glittering in the early afternoon sun. Only the crows were silent, silent and watchful: they alone knew of the carrion rotting in the dressing room.

One of the officers, a young man by the name of Turner, an open-faced, golden-haired, good-hearted man, looked at the beauty around him with appreciation and delight. The other officers had gone on ahead, only Turner was dawdling and taking his time. 'I could be the last man on earth,' he said to himself. 'Or the first. These are truly paradisiacal surroundings.' A butterfly flitted across his path, a languid yellow fluttering presence. It reminded him of home, and he felt inexplicably happy.

He hurried to catch up with the others, and he was out of breath by the time he arrived at the house. It was a party of four: Dunbar, Forbear, Kennedy and Turner. They went in silence from room to room. The great wooden door that led from the veranda was shut, but not bolted. Sparrows chattered in the eaves, and the smell of roses, of the red and white roses, wafted in from the bushes that fronted the house.

They went to the downstairs drawing room, with its polished floorboards and patterned wallpaper and cheerful chintz curtains. A collection of scarabs was set in a glass case. A faint and unfamiliar odour clung to the room, compounded of the heady fragrance of patchouli and the smell of dung. They looked at each other strangely but remained silent; something in the room discouraged speech.

The dining room, where they went next, had a good collection of china in those days – it was of course pilfered in the interregnums of ownership. Oranges and apples were set in a glass bowl upon the dining table, which was covered with a tablecloth of fine lace. The room was as the missionary's wife, Mrs Cockerell, had left it, calm and quiet, a place of repose. The officers examined the paintings that hung on the whitewashed walls. (The wallpaper, brought all the way from England, had been sufficient only for the parlour.) There were some weak watercolours, executed by the late Mrs Cockerell, of the hills, of the snows, of the house itself. Marcus had installed a print by Beardsley from the 'Salomé' series. It looked odd and out of place in that tranquil room. They stared at it without comment, and then proceeded to climb up the wooden staircase, their tread becoming suddenly more military, more formal.

Dunbar, Forbear, Kennedy and Turner. Turner was already feeling a strange chill, a sort of cold pallor, descending upon him. His left eyelid was flickering, and the golden hair on his arms and chest was all on edge, not from fright, but the presentiment of something bad and final. They did not bother to knock when they entered the first bedroom: they stood in formation and entered in a quick sudden movement, like men who are already expecting the worst.

That was Marcus's bedroom, which he rarely used. The old washerwoman, the mother of the beautiful beloved of the young sepoy, was a clever, cunning, practical soul, who had come with her parents from the plains when the cantonment first recruited staff. After the slaughter of the two Englishmen, she had carefully brought in all the washing and ironing, some of which had lain with her for months. Of course she did not leave it in the dressing room, where properly it should have been kept, but the fact of its orderly and reassuring presence as a tidy heap on Munro's bed led the military court at Ranikhet which heard the case to rule out the involvement of the servants in the tragedy. With a combination of haste and distaste the tribunal arrived at the overriding conclusion that it was death by misadventure, thus effectively ruling out any suggestion of foul play.

After they had nosed their way through the clothes, and stared without comment at the black candles on the mantelpiece, and leafed through the slender volumes of verse with long dedications (one of them was even dedicated to Marcus), they moved on to the other bedroom. They had sensed by now where the evil lay, but they were all delaying confronting it. Munro's room was in order, the servants had tidied it up, although superstition and hatred kept them from pilfering the money, the valuables and oddments they could so easily have made their own. It had trunks full of old correspondence, letters to and from the members of the Order of the Golden Dawn, and to a break-away group which Munro's great-aunt, a renowned spiritualist of her time, had briefly headed. These convoluted, contentious epistles were later to be puzzled over endlessly and to no avail at the military court that heard the case.

They proceeded next to the study, where behind the window,

beyond the curtain, I am suspended in time, exiled from the flux of eternity. The sunset arrives early in winter: it is a spectacular, bravura show – all glistening snow and pink and orange light before the twilight and the darkness set in. They congregated at my window to take the splendour in, and the sacred snow peaks of the Himalayas gazed at them in the certainty of beauty and wisdom in the kingdom of earth.

Then the shadows began to set in, just a hint of the advancing evening. In that suggestion of darkness they hurriedly examined the room, not lingering by the grinning skull that sat upon the mahogany desk, noting the presence of the carved pentagram, the richly bound Book of Secrets upon its ornate stand, the Chinese opium pipe that lay in the drawer. Many things they ignored, for they had understood the portent of what they had seen, and they did not want to see any more. Tight-lipped, they moved to the dressing room.

They had to break the door of the dressing room open. The four of them pushed it in, it didn't require much force. Of course the smell had already warned them of what to expect. I am queasy about decay, it does not appeal to me, involving as it does a breakdown and degeneration of energies. Yet something compelled me to enter the room with them, although strictly speaking it was none of my business. Perhaps I felt an empathy with that man Turner – he was so vulnerable; I wanted to protect him from what lay ahead.

The sprawled-out bodies were the ugliest things I ever saw. The word evil does not belong to our plane, but I have to use it to explain to you what lay within those four walls. Just the smell was enough to drive anyone mad, composed as it was of fear and putrefaction. It is only natural for the flesh to decay, it is process;

but Munro's decomposing face was caught in such a grimace of pain and anger, it held such a hideous monstrosity of expression, that it negated by its very existence every notion of the moral life as humans recognise it. Kennedy succumbed and vomited right there at the door, but the other three continued gamely in.

The odd thing was that although Marcus had lost an arm and Munro was mauled in the face, their bodies, lying in grotesque operatic postures of tragic demise, were in dramatically different stages of decomposition. Munro, whose contorted face was a blurred and bloodied mass of flesh, had also deteriorated in the body. A sort of slime enveloped him and I could glimpse maggots darting through places where the flesh had broken, making merry between his fingers, cavorting at his arched-out elbows. In his arms lay Marcus, who looked as though he were merely asleep; his wry, ironic face was pulled into an expression of sorrowful understanding, the even features, although ravaged by boredom and dissipation, maintaining still a strange internal composure. The busy spiders that bedevil our hills had spun cobwebs upon his head, as though to compensate his golden tresses for the grey they would never see.

'Now, the King of Terrors being Death, it is hard indeed to look it in the face, so Mankind has created a host of phantastic masks.' These words were spoken in a soft sibilant whisper. It was undeniably Munro's voice, the theatrical, slightly phoney voice he used while declaiming the Mysteries, as he used to while standing atop the chair in his study haranguing the group. I heard him, I saw his lips move, and the soldiers heard him too.

Kennedy was vomiting in a corner of the room: he heaved and retched and heaved. Dunbar opened the window and leaned out to breathe in the fresh air; Forbear put a handkerchief to his mouth and examined the bodies as clinically as he could, noted the time by his stopwatch, and jotted down a few other observations for the official records. And poor Turner, who so short a time ago had concluded that nature and this world were in happy, symphonic harmony, looked up at the dark oak rafters and saw therein the shadow of his own death.

A year to the day, he hanged himself from the rafters of the barracks at Bareilly, where he was then posted. The last thought in his mind remained what he had just seen – the maggot twisting in the corner of what had been Munro's mouth, the diamond glistening at his shirt cuff. Kennedy was drowned at sea just a little way out of Bombay harbour – some thought he had committed suicide. Dunbar became a man of the cloth and later emigrated to Australia. Forbear became a general and a man of great substance. For all of them this moment had somehow changed their lives. I felt a great sorrow and helplessness as I saw them, human, vulnerable, afraid.

The sepoys were called in. They wrapped the bodies in gunny-bags and removed them from the house. They were given a discreet burial, but something in them festered still and demanded cleansing. Seven days after the burial, lightning struck the graveyard and rent the tombstone on Munro's grave to pieces. Marcus's grave had no tombstone, for the mason who had carved Munro's marble epitaph had himself fallen down a ravine the very day he had completed his labours. At the insistence of the priest they were moved to unconsecrated ground, and the winter frost and snow soon obliterated all traces of their existence.

The army decided to requisition the house, to scotch the strange and disturbing rumours that had quite naturally come into circulation.

The Colonel of the regiment, a man called Osborne, moved into the big house, although it was inconvenient for him in every possible way. The imprint of that violence could not be so easily erased. The house continued to nurture an anger, a sullen quiet, a waiting. Strange things began to happen – at least they looked strange to the Colonel. I could hear him sigh late into the night from my vantage point behind the window, from where I contemplated the glimmering snow peaks, embraced by the dark of the winter night. Osborne had seen the world, he was too old to be afraid, but he knew that something was not right in the house. He was alert; he was attuned to trouble.

The dressing room which had witnessed the dreadful deaths was a small room containing two almirahs and a large dressing table, the mirror of which, originally imported from England, had cracked and been replaced by a locally produced mirror which had misted over. Osborne avoided looking at the mirror; he would adjust his cravat or comb his hair in the bedroom, or in the bathroom where the brilliant white light from the snow peaks rendered the gleaming window panes almost as effective as the blotchy mirror in the dressing room.

One day I found him examining his countenance with a deep and morose interest. His left eye was stained a dark purple, and vivid red welts shone like stigmata on his neck and arms. I wondered what the matter was: he did not have the aura of illness, although a field of anxiety and resignation was beginning to attach itself to him. The regimental doctor was summoned, but he was as puzzled as I was. He concluded that Osborne had been bitten by bedbugs and that the mattress and bedding should be aired. He left after prescribing a bottle of Sloan's liniment for the alleviation of the Colonel's woes; it was of course another kind of bottle in which Osborne sought and found solace. The servants were scolded for their negligence, and the room was aired and cleaned and smoked with pine-gum, which made me weak and faint and sick.

That night the Colonel consumed a full bottle of claret with a speed and ferocity that surprised me. It was a cold February evening, and the wind was blowing through the old house with a venomous hiss, at a frequency which disturbed my equilibrium. Perhaps it is a past-life phobia, but I hate the February winds in this house. They are malicious, malignant, they throw me back to a time when I was trapped in a long tunnel, lit by a blinding white light, which seemed harmonious at first, but later I was racked by just such a wind, mindless and intent upon passage.

Osborne was smelling strongly of Sloan's liniment. It is a repellent smell; it troubles me even more than the gum arabic. What with the wind whispering like a crazed creature, and the smoke from the fire that was spreading through the room like a pall because of the strong overhead winds, which were preventing the chimneys from functioning effectively – between these things I felt well and truly trapped.

I have learnt from bitter experience that there is no solace or relief in philosophising – it only exacerbates the wounds of my fractured experience. Still, something in that cold chill, lifeless February day made me cry out at the injustice of my situation. It is terrible to be suspended in time and space, without a body, without a context, ignorant of the reasons and circumstance that have led to this strange exile, this cruel isolation. Knowledge is no consolation, nor is it any comfort to be at a vantage point where the synchronicity of things, their ebb and flow, and the current of linear time, are all so clearly visible.

I feel so unutterably lonely, trapped behind the curtain, venturing out sometimes around the house, or as far as the front gate. What brought me here, who left me here? My vision and understanding are only exterior. I can gaze at this passing show of humans, and watch their follies and frailties, but they can so rarely sense or see me. We belong to different worlds, and the bubble of accident that blankets me also isolates me from contact with other spheres and channels. I dream incessantly of the dryad that lives in the deodar tree. Her dimension may in some terms be approximate to my own, but I fear I do not possess the courage to make that journey. The hopes that I have nursed for so long are all I have; I do not have the conviction to put them to the test. I know already it is never to be: why then test the inevitable?

But I digress again. I did not know then, in that cold February evening, that Osborne would pick up his gun from its perch in the panelled study wall and venture into the blustery twilight, successfully shoot at a rabbit, rape a hill woman returning from the forest with a bale of grass and fodder balanced upon her head, and, after taking his satisfaction of her, shoot himself through the temple and die. He lay on the bridle-path to Ranneekhet, the bridle-path lined with the red wounds of the flowering rhododendron, still smelling of Sloan's liniment, his open eyes observing the heavens, his spirit fled in panic to some discordant dimension, his bruised eye and the red welts upon his body now destined never to heal.

Such passages always cause me pain. Presences arrive, from other planes, other existences, to observe, welcome and aid the process of transmigration. I look at them wistfully, even with a certain envy. When, I wonder to myself, shall I be reclaimed? Who is the one, the friend from the past, who will come and assist me to cross over?

Osborne's wife and his young daughter who had died at sixteen came forth to greet him They had not been warned, they were utterly unprepared for his arrival. I shuddered in sympathy as I observed their consternation, for they could not find him, he was lost in that same cold tunnel of light which I had so vividly remembered when I smelt the Sloan's liniment. It could have been Osborne's precognition or mine, but the trauma of his severance hurt me, sorrowed me, goaded me to remember my own betrayal: but as usual I could recollect nothing.

Despair and dislocation were the emotions that clung to Osborne's body as it lay on the side of the bridle-path, where the pebbles and shale were covered by a rain of pine needles. As the dawn broke over the Himalayas, the soft blotch of blood on his temple, the welts on his face, his bruised eye showed not at all as the morning light caught the gossamer tendrils of an immaculate web which the busy spiders at their ceaseless task had begun even as he stumbled and fell to the ground, and the report of the bullet echoed through the silent hills, scaring the rabbits away.

He was buried in consecrated ground, absolved of suicide; it was an accident. The house, empty again, slumped back into inertia. I returned to my internal time, suspended without event behind the curtains, watching the eternal snows of the Himalayas as they glimmered from rose to red to white to orange, purple, blue and then grey again. This was the vision of humans, but in my own way of seeing I could perceive many other things. I could see the scorn, the mocking arrogance, of the burgeoning mountain presences as they forced their way through the earth with the vitality of young things. I could see their boredom, their impatience with time. The fog that swirls around the Himalayas is the memory of the sea: its playful presence is a shadow impersonation summoned by the fish, fossils and sand that once accommodated water and brine and the ocean's mysteries, not rock and ice.

When Father Benedictus arrived in Ranikhet, he was a guest at the parsonage. He was the author of two modern and much-acclaimed books on theology, and he had come to the Himalayas to escape from the tedium of the intense controversy his latest book had generated, especially within the Church. The parsonage was in the cantonment, and Father Benedictus did not like it there, it was simply too neat and orderly for him. 'They have managed to cut up the mountains and set them into straight lines,' he said, and he did his best to keep away from the set routine and defined regimen of military life.

The Father was a man given to long rambling walks. He collected butterflies, and folklore, and was garnering material for a book upon the folk tales of Kumaon and Nepal. I tried to explain to him, in the course of our many conversations, how the butterfly is the most sensitive of creatures: it accommodates in its fragile frame many transients, souls between lives, unfinished karmas, spirits seeking sustenance and substance. When they die their due death, their passage is spontaneous and free of conflict, but when these adepts at metamorphosis are caught, framed and pinned to a base, and then confined to an airless case or examined through a magnifying glass, they release a nervous energy quite unsettling for those attuned to these emanations.

It was on one of his butterfly expeditions that Father Benedictus chanced upon the house. When, in the course of a walk that broke into a long run, his white beard waving like a flag as he panted in pursuit of the species Lepidoptera, he turned the final bend which leads to this house, and thereafter past the two thickets of bamboo that frame the asymmetrical white triangle of Nanda Devi, he was a man enchanted, enslaved, entrapped. The view from the house, the spread of hill and mountain and forest, man's realm, which gave way in one breathtaking instant to snow and sky, God's realm, the aching beauty and joy of that view, held him in thrall.

Instantly he sought the permission of the new Colonel to stay there for a six-month. The permission was hastily granted, and Benedictus moved out of the cantonment into the enormous, empty, waiting shell of this edifice. He knew nothing of its history; people in the hills have a habit of instinctively clamping up about such things without reason, while being voluble and even loquacious about other matters. The subject of this house has always commanded silence, and its serene and pleasant proportions betray no secrets and tell no tales to the outsider.

Yet it was not as though he had been lacking in observation. 'This garden has so much vigour,' he had said to himself, that first fateful day when he chanced upon the house, 'it has so much vigour that it is *contra natura*.'

Night after night I would watch Benedictus settle down with his booty of butterflies, like a child with candy. He had moved his books and papers and cases of captive insects to the mahogany desk in the study, the same which had been graced by the small skull that doubled as paperweight and blood cup. Every evening he would pore over the moths, the butterflies and the skippers, the caterpillars, the chrysalis and the imagos, as though seeking in their growth and grace some form of personal redemption. He would examine them short-sightedly through a magnifying glass: the head, the thorax, the abdomen, the complex eyes, the simple eyes. Books and butterflies would lie piled on the table as he taxed his intellect with classification and categories, species and sub-species. He could not hear them scream.

The scream of the butterfly is the saddest sound in this world. Ghosts, spirits, butterflies, bats and, I believe, vampires exist in a mutually receptive auditory sphere. As the bat beats his wings and makes for the butterfly, he can feel the faint frail presence in his pulse. But strategy and subterfuge is the way of the butterfly, it knows well how to betray the very instincts of its predators. The high-pitched grating sound with which it confuses the bat reverberates at a frequency inaudible to humans. These screams, these keening wails, are accompanied by a tangible terror, despair and desolation.

Life as the butterfly knows it is a fearful quest for nectar. As it peers at the world through the saturated colours of its spectrum, the blues, the violets, the indigos – as through this beauty it registers the threat of the Other – as it hoops and dives and beats its wings in a frenzy of fear and panic, it creates a flutter in my field, it resonates through my centre for an unreasonable time. It is not that I am sentimental: butterflies just have that effect on me.

It was agony to share the room with Father Benedictus: his orgiastic delight in decapitating the innocent creatures drove me wild with rage. I decided to move out, and even accommodated myself in an outhouse near the main gate for some time. But the length of my inexplicable imprisonment in this dimension has rendered me a creature of habit, and I found that I missed my little corner. Then there was the view – I had got used to the mountain presences that loomed before me day and night. And so I returned to my old haunt, and accosted Father Benedictus there.

I discovered to my utter surprise that he could see and recognise me. In the language that is beyond words, Father Benedictus addressed me with respect and affection. It is rare enough for us to encounter any sympathy within a human mode, leave alone communication. Benedictus's understanding amazed and delighted me. I had already begun my impassioned plea on behalf of the butterflies; the Father listened intently, his wise white beard shaking in motion with his head as he focused on my thoughts. He had the capacity to listen and to understand. With a sigh and a gentle shake of his voluminous white beard which cascaded like a waterfall all the way to his knees he accepted my point of view, and moving to the table let free the day's harvest of iridescent creatures into the scented night air, where a field of evening primrose released its fragrance to welcome them home.

Benedictus lit up a cheroot, observing wryly that an addiction to tobacco did not behove a man of the cloth. We sat together in companionable silence, exchanging thoughts and ideas through darts and quivers of intuition. It was the first friendship of my life, and that night, as I watched the snow mountains shimmering softly in the moonlight, I pitied their solitude and separateness.

I learnt a lot from Father Benedictus. In the course of our many conversations, which loomed late into the long night, he taught me the art of verbalisation, organised thought, the language of humans. Words are difficult quantities for us to comprehend. They are shadows themselves, elusive approximations, but I mastered them. That mastery gave me joy and satisfaction and also body; it earthed me, grounded me, made me human-like. Words create immense complications, but they can give life to the most incorporeal things. They became a heady intoxication, an addiction. For me, words will always remain associated with the wraith of cheroot smoke which encircled our conversations. In fact you could say that I did not exist before Benedictus entered the sphere of my unbroken observations, and, with the spirit of words, put a hat upon the hollow head of my self-hood, so to speak.

The range of education I received from Father Benedictus was encyclopaedic, and yet it was marked by the most alarming and incongruous gaps: but then I believe this is a frequent misadventure with all knowledge, a necessary hazard in the arbitrary enlarging of consciousness.

Sometimes I think that perhaps this house is my body. In his customary patient manner, Father Benedictus once explained that humans know themselves by means of vision, balance and the functioning of the sustaining organs; the thread on the beads being sentience, or the sense of self-perception. Well, my window on the world is naught else but this spot, the blinding light of the Himalayas on one side of me, the dark room with forty-two rafters on the other. Yes, this house is my body.

Once, when I was protesting against the miserable fate that left me without visible or material proof of my existence, the Father made this rejoinder: 'The body, like the clothes we wear, is only an emblem of identity, to mark the wearer as such-and-such; these outward accoutrements often serve to conceal more than they reveal. Much deceit and dissimulation hides behind the flowing robes of my cassock. I am after all a human, perhaps not a very wise one. Once, as a young man, when I was in the military, I fancied myself a soldier of the body, eager to combat evil with sword and gun. Of course I discovered soon enough that the real evil lay within, but in those days, when I first donned the tight-fitting uniform of the soldier, I can assure you that I felt quite differently. Assuredly, clothes make the body that constitutes the man, and you, dear spirit, are blessed beyond belief not to be burdened with these millstones!'

He told me of a man he was in correspondence with, a doctor of the mind, called Sigmund Freud, and another, a student of the first, one Carl Jung. 'Our century has mapped the human mind in the way the one before mapped the globe in which we live. But I sometimes fear that this acute spirit of enquiry, this over-dissectiveness, will quite chase the genie out of the bottle, as it were!' he exclaimed, his white beard shaking in consternation at the future of thoughtless mankind.

Father Benedictus was a seeker of knowledge and a skilled interrogator. He drew from me the substance of my extraneous energies, things known and things observed, as also the subtler memories of unformulated associations, reminders and echoes, besides of course gauging the mechanical constraints and conditionalities of my existence. In return, he attempted to explain the contradictions of human life to me. He would use the framework of his friend Carl Jung, who posited – how effortlessly I could now use the burden of words! – who posited the existence of the Religious Instinct, a counterpole to the three biological drives of the primitive instincts. It was this Higher Self that Father Benedictus sought, but he was in despair that he would ever find it, for the call of instinct controlled his complex nature.

I tried to grope beneath the words into the mind of the man before me. I encountered a physicality, a sensuality, a primal joyous strength; and then I met with the resistance of a powerful counter-pull. I saw before me the image of a great iceberg, a floating mountain of ice, such as I had never conceived or encountered. This iceberg was gliding determinedly through a cold northern sea, and, although the winds that blew so forcefully in that dream landscape pulled and urged it in one direction, the submerged mass of its being, its true self, guided it to another goal, another shore. So it was with the mind of Father Benedictus.

We spent many weeks together, dismantling barriers, increasing our understanding. He would list the confusions of mankind for me. There were philosophers who doubted if the existence of the physical, objective world could be proved – a suggestion present in St Augustine, discussed at length by Kant, and present in Leibnitz's windowless monads. As you see, the Father taught me well. Our time passed in talking and laughter and merriment.

As the flames shuddered and the embers crackled in the huge fireplace, the ill-constructed chute would periodically regurgitate a shower of soot and dirt. Sometimes, when the wood was damp, the haze from the Father's cheroots would bump into the smoke escaping the hearth. Then Benedictus would throw open the windows, from where the cool Himalayan wind would sweep through the room in a playful dance, and a joyousness, a gentle certainty, would fill up the room, a sort of unvoiced laughter. Benedictus could do that to a room.

The Father told me of different aspects of his world, of which I had no conception. He talked to me of the sport of archery, of the arrow of intent as it leaves the tautly strung bow of the mind and alights upon its object. He even had a painted target, which he had constructed himself, set up in the tennis field, and fashioned some bows and arrows with the green and supple bamboo that guards the gates of the house.

I could see him from my spot by the window, as, time and again, he hit his target with the unerring aim of the initiate. But I saw what he did not see – I saw a monstrous man, with bulging biceps, and a terrible, lascivicious gaze, alight from a palanquin and examine my friend the good Father in a foaming paroxysm of rage. Father Benedictus continued with his game of archery, his mind and body intent in joint purpose. The apparition returned to its palanquin, which was carried by strange maidens with distorted faces and feet that protruded backwards, leaving behind it a procession of dogs which stayed to observe Father Benedictus at play with his arrows.

At night they set up a profound howling, but the Father assured me that this was quite in order, for canines are compelled by the nature of their biology to bay at the moon. Then, in the depth of the night, we heard a cock crow, and the Father started in his sleep. These were not good omens, they foretold disturbance, but I did not tell the Father of my intuitions of disaster.

A few months after Father Benedictus moved into the house, a strange smell began to emanate from the dressing room, the one where Marcus and Munro had met their gory end. The Father took to leaving the window open, to let in the fresh mountain breezes, which tended to be cold and capricious at that time of the year. The February wind has always driven me to a deep recess of internal despair, and it would make its way around the house, sauntering insolently from room to room, banging doors, opening windows, sending the Father's papers flying, sometimes straight into the fireplace.

When he shut the window, the smell returned again, stronger than before. We do not have a sense of smell in our dimension, because we do not possess the host of associations and memories that are half the function of smell. Instead we have a corresponding sense, one for which I have no words, which approximates in a non-olfactory way to the degree of energy or entropy of a place or object, or to the form and function of a creature's active pheromones. Dona Rosa for instance (I hope you who hear me have not forgotten her, for she is the reason I am assuming human voice), Dona Rosa smelt in my world of flowers in bloom, of lust, of the ripe moment in time before impregnation, when great beauty sits waiting, ready for its own perpetuation.

The dressing room smelt of suppuration, of decay, of rot without renewal. Father Benedictus would hold a handkerchief doused in lavender-water to his face before crossing over to go to the bathroom. The process of excretion in humans is so very cumbersome and primitive that it causes me both amazement and pity. Words, too, could in my world be understood as a form of excreta, for they exist only after the act of cognition, as dead symbols of the mind's working.

Of course, I could not understand or formulate these emotions before Father Benedictus gave me the gift of speech. The nuances and exactitudes of emotion, they did not exist for me, and the measuring and retailing of thought held no meaning. There were only undifferentiated clods and clumps of reaction – attract or repel, accept or reject, yes or no. Now, burdened by knowledge, how I long to repossess that state of grace, far from the betrayals and uncertainties of the ineffectual, masquerading life of words.

The thunderbox was cleaned by a low-caste sweeper, whose job it was to carry out the offending rejections of Father Benedictus's digestive system to some suitably distant spot, from where they could once again refertilise the earth. The Father was too gentle ever to scold anyone, but he reproached the sweeper, the boy Ramu, for being careless with his duties. This reproach from that kindest of men so hurt Ramu that he ran away to his village in Pithoragarh, four days' journey from Ranikhet in those days, and for a full week there was nobody in the house of the correct hierarchical status to clear the thunderbox.

The Father began using the other washroom, the disused one behind the guest room. However, he could not bear to change his bedroom, for he had got habituated to the white patch of snow mountain that was visible from his pillow first thing in the morning.

Then the flies began appearing, hundreds and thousands of them, clusters and clouds of flies; they buzzed and hummed in the dressing room with a manic intensity that completely disturbed my orientation. How different they were from the spirits of my beloved butterflies, questing for the nectar of life – these scavengers, these vectors, these feasters on decay! Father Benedictus told me, in his scholastic, even pedantic way, about the nature and purpose of the dipterans, how, being sensitive to process, alert to decay, they are designated by the greater vision of nature to break down and redistribute organic matter. One could say that therein lay their karma.

Perhaps they had been summoned to the dressing room by the memories of the maggots which had feasted upon Marcus and Mad Munro, through all the progressive stages of rigor and putrefaction. Or else some trick of time had assigned them this phantom task, reasserted the fierce forces that fought forgetting, denied the cleansing mountain breeze and the forgiveness of the sun. Father Benedictus too sensed the purpose of their congregation – they had come, we both understood, to assert something that he denied.

They would not leave even when all the doors and windows were left open: they continued to buzz and swoon in dementia within the confines of that little room. The servants were summoned from the quarters, and a conference was held upon how to cope with the menace. It was decided to smoke the enemy out. Pine resin and gum arabic were lit in earthen containers and left to smoulder in the dressing room. The flies did not depart, but instead congealed and coagulated into a small, dense, huddled mass. An intrepid servant, one who knew about these things, muttered some mantras and then wrapped the writhing, buzzing globule into a black cloth and carried it out. The next day some of them returned, but they seemed diminished both in numbers and spirit.

For some strange reason the gum arabic made me de-escalate in consciousness. I found myself wandering in that old forlorn dimension, in that familiar telescope of hurt from where a hostile white light pushed me even further into an unknown abyss. Father Benedictus had told me of the region of limbo, a place of neither salvation nor damnation. Perhaps I had been confined to limbo, that white tunnel without remembrance. Somehow I crawled out of that area of non-being, recovered my sentience, invoked my strength. I wanted to leave, to go away from the house, but I felt an inertia, a sweet resignation, that prevented me from any measure of initiative.

The Father, in the meanwhile, was pensive and troubled. He had taken to fasting, and would eat nothing. He would sit by the draughty fire, a sprig of basil in his palm, and stroke his long flowing white beard in an abstracted manner. Sometimes, to distract himself, he would lovingly examine the boxes of mutilated moths, their mimic eyes staring at him in anger and defeat, pinned as they were to the velvet-layered glass case, rather than the confines of the velvety night where they had once belonged. Strategies of deception are essential to survival, but the Father was too noble, too sure in his God-given goodness, to search for one. His antipode had found him out, he had to surrender or else flee to escape it.

Late into the night, as he was sitting before the last of the glowing embers, I overheard the Father talking to himself. 'There are two opposite and equal errors about the nature of the Devil,' he said. 'The first is to disbelieve in his existence. The other is to believe, and be drawn into an excessive and unhealthy interest. He himself is well pleased by both errors, that of the materialist as well as that of the magician.' He sighed, his beard rippling with the long-drawn breath, and closed his eyes as though in great pain.

Weak, dejected and exhausted as I was, I staggered (which is to indicate that my energies fluctuated with every forward movement) to where Father Benedictus was sitting and tugged at his cassock. He looked at me in surprise, as though I had shaken him from some very distant world, and then bestowed on me a smile of such infinite love and unutterable gentleness that I was restored, renewed, regenerated. I felt soothed and settled by his aura of strength, surrounded for that moment by the peace of acceptance and surrender. Then I left him alone and returned to my spot near the window, where, from behind the curtain, I contemplated the cruel jest that had positioned me so tenuously in the scheme of things.

Although he had taught me about the glyphs of language, Father Benedictus and I did not communicate through the medium of words, or imagery, or symbols. We participated instead in a sort of osmosis, where we permeated each other's consciousness and experienced thus a complete and uncomplicated understanding at every level. We both knew when we met that last time that the two of us were not destined to collide again in our particular shapes, spheres and emanations. A sorrow passed between us that our friendship had been so brief.

Suddenly a wooden chair, the same chair that had been the

favourite podium of Munro, atop which he had delivered his mad discourses, the chair which stood before the mahogany desk, beside the fireplace, this chair rose up in the air as though propelled by a powerful jet of water. It was pushed up, not pulled, and floated uneasily in a clumsy defiant movement, the forces of gravity beckoning, the ego of its instigator hurling it towards the ceiling. It stood suspended in the middle of the room for some ten minutes; both of us watched astonished as it came crashing down on the polished floor, where its four legs now stood, inversely facing the painted rafters on the ceiling. Then, with a sudden, jerky, determined movement, it corrected itself and stood upright again, facing us, moored to the floor, in conjunction with gravity.

Father Benedictus betrayed no surprise. 'The only way to drive out the Devil, when he does not yield to texts or scripture, is to jeer and flaunt him; for his is a proud spirit, which cannot endure scorn,' he said, in his usual gentle and even tone.

Then he bade me leave. 'I have now to exorcise the source of this evil,' he told me gravely. 'To do so I must further evoke it. Go away, far away, beyond harm and danger. Do not return until I call for you. Goodbye.' Without a word of farewell I left for the gatehouse, where upon arrival I collapsed into an insensate void. When I came to I sensed a great body of pain, compassion and contiguous pain, and I knew at once that I had to return to the house.

Father Benedictus was no longer alive: his spirit had departed the body. His flesh was seated on the chair, the same chair which had gravitated to the ceiling and danced about the room. His face was calm, composed, mildly inquisitive, and he had his spectacles on. Although he was dead, his voice lingered in the room in the heard tones of the language of men. It spoke to me softly, even shyly. 'The past belongs only to the past,' it said, 'and the future – behold! It is free and fearless.'

He had only just departed from his body, the orifices were still closing their apertures. A crowd of hungry spirits, displaced like me from their natural host-bodies, were jostling around the radiant cast-off sheath of his body, but it held such residual powers that they were hesitant to enter. The resonance, the after-shadow, of the Father's spirit had levitated to a spot approximately where the chair had hung suspended the previous day; he was excited and eager as a schoolboy at a picnic. Never had I encountered a human more eager to shed his mortal coil.

A young man in a cotton shift came forth to welcome him; he was awkward and hesitant and wore the face of an angel. And then the roof of the house opened out: it vanished and an army of angel appeared, with cornets and trumpets and rolls and peals of thunder.

Cherubim and seraphim greeted him with smiles of abysmal sadness. A tremor of relief communicated itself from the Father's soul to me: the heavens were in order, just as he had been told they would be. But the relief was accompanied by a sense of let-down, of disappointment: it is the misfortune of the human race that they can reach only those heavens they can conceive or aspire to. The joyous sound of harps filled the room; the notes trilled and rose and fell even as the cold wind blew through the faulty chute. A shower of soot fell from the chimney into the fireplace, and suddenly a dancing swarm of butterflies swam in from the open window and battered itself against the inert body which had housed the soul of my best friend.

It was a sight I can never forget: the sky above radiant with a chiaroscuro vision of heaven, which changed before the venturing spirit into a void of spinning stars and glimmering galaxies, and the yellow butterflies splattered like fallen flowers upon the foaming river of Father Benedictus's beard.

On a distant shore I could see a woman that Father Benedictus had loved and left. She was naked, she was asleep on a couch, her stomach swelled in the last stage of pregnancy. She did not know that her lover and the father of her unborn child was departing this world: and yet she was wary and watchful, she knew something was not as it should be. The Father had forgotten her, forgotten his doubts, forgotten the reminder of his life, the residue of his battling passions, the male foetus that nestled in her warm womb. The boy would never know his father, never know the tall man with the white beard who was even now facing an epiphany of misunderstanding.

I too was orphaned by his death. I still grieve the pain of his departure, although by giving me the gift of words and language he did me a disservice – he bound me to schemes and symbols and dimensions which my insubstantial and incorporeal self should never have entered. Human affairs are an amazing web of trivialities, convoluted by interpersonal alignments into a weft and woof of longing and despair. This captivity is all the more cruel for one like myself, a castaway from an unremembered past. How I wish, sometimes, that the Father had left me alone, content and complete in my exile.

After Father Benedictus's death, I fell into a strange condition of apathy. Although he had taught me much, his lessons had taken me on a path of no return. He had acclimatised me to this human world to a degree that negated my actual condition. For many years the house lay empty, and I fluttered behind the curtain, suspended in a void. I was getting used to the absurdity of my condition, to the impossibility of it, when Dona Rosa and her friend Wolcott embarked upon the long voyage across oceans and continents to this lonely spot in our hills.

The patient reader who has given ear to my ramblings may pardon my discursive, wandering prose. My primary narrative, the subject and focus of my memories, is after all not Marcus or Munro or even the good Father Benedictus. My muse, the object of my meditations, is Dona Rosa, she of the rose-red lips, she of the wandering heart, she of the beguiling eyes and bewitching smile. Oh, Dona Rosa, as you sit before the window in the glowing sunset, as the advancing shadows redefine the planes of your beautiful face, my heart stops as I sight you and I beseech the fates to halt the moment against the tides of time. In an agony of remembrance I relive my hours with you, in the memory which is the prerogative of words.

Dona Rosa was beautiful beyond belief. There was a force field of energy around her that was uniquely her own – a compound of certainty and shyness which penetrated all her actions. Why I had to love her so I do not know, but you will understand what I mean when I say that she was incredibly attractive in my dimension. Vitality emanated from her in sparks and starbursts, it lay scattered at her feet like a carpet of light, it created a field of unquestioning force and dancing matter around her. Things bowed to her command – doors, tables, chairs, the apple that she ate, the shoe that she wore. In short, she was magical.

As for Wolcott, he had, in imitation of certain current books he had read, vowed himself to blood-consciousness, not head-consciousness, and to the absolute and immediate fulfilment of every mental and physical impulse. He was shallow, he was stupid, and yet she was drawn to him as though to a magnet. Dona Rosa's attraction to unstable friends stemmed both from her great power of compassion and her unhealthy interest in the world of the spirit, in the paths frequented by poets, dreamers and madmen. No wonder, then, that she ensorcelled the weak and was constantly caught in a trap of her own making.

Beauty is a form of intelligence and grace, and Laura's magic lay sheerly in her beauty. But my poor Dona Rosa was persuaded that she had the tools and powers of the magical world at her command. That fool and masquerader, Captain Wolcott, her lover and partner in deception, was himself convinced that his paramour was heiress to the psychic lineage of Cleopatra and Helen of Troy, not to speak of Isis, Lilith and the Whore of Babylon.

Dona Rosa, needless to say, was extremely flattered by this interpretation of her past, and had gathered up a jamboree of past-life experiences. She could clearly remember the wails of her handmaidens as she was bitten by the asps. When a bee stung her on the cheek, she bore it stoically – it was nothing compared to the kiss of those vipers. As Helen of Troy, she remembered the launching of the thousand ships, and even Wolcott had to point out the improbability of this situation, given that Helen had already fled with Paris to Troy at that juncture.

'I can see it all in my mind's eye,' my darling Dona said airily, 'and besides, I can tell you it wasn't easy being the daughter of Nemesis and the sister of Clytemnestra!' Non-sequiturs came naturally to her, as did every form of vanity, folly and self-deception. She would never know that in the birth before this one she had been a seamstress's assistant, a small stout woman with a lame foot and an alcoholic brother who stole her savings. She had died of typhoid on Christmas Eve, and her last dream had been of great beauty and the privileges that came thereof, the life of the grand ladies who came to the shop, with their backs and their bosoms bussed up in lace and luxury. And indeed the recording angel had granted her this wish. If she was not given discretion, well, she had never asked for it.

I found her, late one evening, attired in an absurd set of gauzy shimmering veils, her lovely breasts goose-pimpled in the cold, the erect nipples big as berries. Captain Wolcott, on the contrary, was fully clothed from head to foot. He had on an undershirt and underwear, socks and shoes, scarf and scarf-pin. Not a breath of cold could penetrate his armour. He stared at her appreciatively, at the perfect body beneath the veils of diamanté, blue and green and violet.

'Hurry up please, I'm cold!' Dona Rosa said plaintively, upon which her lover counselled her to be patient, or she would drive away the great powers that controlled the universe. 'Besides, we have to practise, we have to get it exactly right, my darling,' he told her, in his gravelly, seductive voice, which I knew was one of the things she admired most about him.

As for me, I did not have a voice at all, I could only whisper deep into her soul, but even if she heard me, which she could when she was not distracted by the cold, or by the burden of that silly man's unending instructions, she could not see me, she could not visualise me; and so, in my desperation, I had to enter the body of that charlatan Wolcott, a vehicle I found distasteful in the extreme.

The gift of words, the inappropriate legacy with which my friend Benedictus had burdened me, had rendered me increasingly alienated from my state of disembodiment. Selfhood can be defined only by boundaries, and I had none. I was possessed only of limitations, restrictions and negative attributes. The limbo in which I exist, the contradictions of non-being, were all the more hurtful in the face of Dona Rosa's vibrant physicality, the living stream of her blood, the pounding of her heart, the exuberant singing of her pulse. When I was with her I experienced a desperate desire to escape from the no mans' land of my confinement and become triumphantly manifest. The stealthy infiltration of Captain Wolcott, the convoluted conditionalities of being a succubus, were no substitute for the satisfactions of the human state.

'Hurry up please, I'm cold,' she said again, upon which Captain Wolcott opened the capacious bottom drawer of the old mahogany desk, and extracted a sort of horned crown of gilt and wood. Dona Rosa's veils of diamanté and gauze shimmered in the dark, they shook with mysterious assurance as she shivered and chattered from the cold. 'The Gnostic mass, my dear . . .' Wolcott murmured, upon which Dona Rosa's dulcet voice broke the silence of the room, where only the fire hissed and the wind blew. 'For one kiss wilt thou be willing to give all; but whosoever gives one particle of dust shall lose all in that hour,' she recited. It had taken her hours to commit the passage to memory.

Wolcott moved forward: there was a look of extreme ceremony and solemnity upon his face, and his heart, his heart where I had positioned myself, was agape with fear and awe and portent. The rustle of silk and tissue and gauze, as slowly, very slowly, he removed the first of the three veils. 'Hurry up please, I'm very cold,' she pleaded.

Captain Wolcott was visibly irritated. 'Here we are, trying to summon the mystic, veiled essence of the feminine, and all you can think of is the cold,' he said, almost spitting out the words in his frustration. 'I tell you, you women are all the same!'

My beautiful Laura's eyes became round and tearful, and with a contrite apology she began again. 'I am the blue-lidded daughter of Sunset. I am the naked brilliance of the voluptuous night sky. To me! To me!' she whispered. With a little twirl and a coy pout, she stood unveiled, naked and vulnerable by the light of the fire. Wolcott took a lance and blessed her with it. 'Love is the Law, Love under Will! Do what thou Wilt shall be the whole of the Law!' he intoned. Inside, I could hear his heart pounding with fear and excitement, he was once again the young boy with the innocent face who could enjoy boiled sweets only if he had stolen them. 'Now to my Phallus shall thee give Suck.'

Dona Rosa bent forward to suit her actions to his words, but he pushed her aside impatiently. 'But first, I shall Adore thee,' he said solemnly, and kneeling down beside her he began passionately sucking her big toe.

'You know, darling,' Dona Rosa said conversationally, 'gout always begins with the big toe. My father had gout, so I know.'

'This really is beyond belief!' Wolcott screamed, as he let go of her toe. 'It's intolerable! You have talent for the prosaic! Never have I met a woman with a more ordinary mind!' Getting up, he stamped his foot upon the wooden boards several times in succession, and stomped out of the room in a passionate sulk.

Dona Rosa sighed and settled her naked form on the rug before the fire. She looked sad and forlorn, like a child that has been reprimanded, like the little girl Laura on those long nights when she and her mother Tatiana waited for her father's tread in the corridor, each in their separate rooms, knowing in their heart of hearts that he would not return until morning.

I felt tender and protective, I wanted to kiss her, to reassure her, but Wolcott had left the room. All her life my Laura had altered and evaded the truth with lies and mysteries and fabrications, and the truth of my emotions was of course quite beyond the scope of her experience.

Love is a strange sentiment, even more elusive in the absence of corporeality. I loved her for the strength of her well-rounded wrists, for the gleam of her teeth when she smiled, for the shower of sparks that fell from her hair when she brushed it. But she could never be material for me, substantial to my world – the zones we occupied were not congruent. I was not flesh and blood, and Wolcott's flesh and blood was not my own. The ache that I felt when I was proximate to her, the sense of incompleteness, the compulsion to hold her, to be touched, acknowledged and made real – these were biological follies; I could not comprehend how they had infected me. There is an image imprinted in my mind: Dona Rosa alone by the window, a slight drizzle in the garden, the fog pushing its way in through the mesh window, the suggestion of a faraway rainbow. The field of energy around Dona Rosa, her sheath, is for some reason quite still: there is an air of reflection and sad repose around us. I love her desperately, I am glad she is here near the window beside me, her hair damp and a little frizzy, her eyes pensive. There is a fire burning in the room, but the wood is damp, as is everything around us. Suddenly the door opens and Wolcott comes in, a cigarette glowing in his fingers, a diamond pin sparkling in his cravat. Her eyes light up, she smiles, the sense of expectancy is dispelled and the electricity returns to her movements. She bares her teeth coquetishly and gives him a long, lingering kiss. And me – as for me, I leap out from behind the curtain and enter Wolcott.

I prayed to the elements that I might somehow penetrate a primary physical dimension. I too wanted a body. Sexuality is an embarrassment for our kind – it is a force our dimension does not comprehend, for, as you may understand, we do not reproduce, not even asexually. Reproduction and the desire for racial immortality is the culprit in the pathetic travesty that humans call love. As though that contemptible Wolcott could understand that noble word! It is nothing but the cunning of the genes in their frenzied search for the Other! And yet, that was precisely what I wanted to do. I wanted to personally and individually possess and penetrate Dona Rosa. I will not say that I did not know even then that this was the highest form of hubris conceivable to my situation.

Both Dona Rosa and Wolcott were fond of drinking: they consumed great quantities of alcohol quite regularly. I loved to watch her drink, observe the loosening of inhibitions, the unleashing of her intuitions. Her hair dishevelled, her eyes a little unfocused, her cheeks flushed – that is how I still cherish her. She was easier to penetrate then, I could access her without Wolcott as an intermediary. He had to remain as an accessory, but only as a cutout or gateway to the sheath of her being. She was so luminous, so complete, so joyous in her self-absorption that I could completely lose myself in her. I could abandon my nebulous barriers so totally that it was only the physical presence of Wolcott as a medium which allowed me even to return to the place from which I had ventured forth.

When Dona Rosa and Wolcott had drunk too much liquor, their consciousness became querulous, cloudy and granular. The drinking and carousing began to spread to the staff. One night there was chaos in the servants' quarters. The cook had lashed the bearer with fifty strokes, not of the whip but of nettles first soaked in water then twined against a supple bamboo cane. Dear spirits of heaven and hell, it must have hurt.

I am not clear about the cause of the troubles, but they began with mutual recriminations and allegations of theft against the head cook's wife by the washerwoman, conveyed imprudently to the cook by the bearer. The lives of the servants are too mired in the fundamental dimension of physical survival to interest me. Besides, they live too far away from my window, they are too complex and too simple, and so I keep my distance from them.

The native Pahari estate-manager, lord and master of the cooks, gardeners, bearers and houseboys, a tall gaunt man called Lohani, came in to mediate the matter with Wolcott and Dona Rosa. The two had carefully kept themselves in a state of blissful ignorance concerning the management of the estate, and even now they were in a hurry to dispose of the manager and resume their daily pleasures without the unpleasant burdens of responsibility.

I was struck by the physical appearance of the estate-manager. He was not entirely of human dimension. Like my friend Benedictus, he had a receptivity to, a connection with, channels other than his own. This was manifested even on the physical scale, in his ears, which were unnaturally large and seemed to take in the slightest auditory disturbance in the room. He wore gleaming gold earrings, and stood tall and proud before his alien masters, not at all intimidated by their airs.

I understood immediately that he was the true guardian spirit of the house, appointed by the mountain manes to prevent the sacred spine of the hill, the dragon's back, from being violated and desecrated by these adventurers. He was a true man, a strong and holy man, he belonged to the forces of equilibrium and reconciliation. Instinctively I cloaked myself from him. I did not wish to be seen or recognised, it was not apt or appropriate. Our worlds were different. He was already familiar with the mysteries of the house. My existence was a necessary gap in his knowledge.

Wolcott and Dona Rosa dismissed him impatiently, enjoining him to do what he pleased in the matter of the servants' quarrel. Wolcott returned to the contemplation of the blank sheet of paper that was to be his next book of poetry, and Dona Rosa to her tarot pack, to the minor arcana, where she confronted the Eight of Wands to defy her fate.

A black kitten wandered into the house from the servants' quarters and settled itself before the fireplace, maintaining a cautious distance from Dona Rosa and Wolcott. Naturally Dona Rosa had to fall in love with it. She named it 'Mishka', and was constantly trying to ingratiate herself with sympathetic sounds and warm saucers of milk. Mishka maintained a studied indifference, and continued to sit by the hearth in perfect contentment.

One day Mishka was afflicted by a bad stomach, and defecated on the rug that lay by the fireplace. This enraged the bearer Sherua, the one who was waging constant war with the head cook. That very afternoon he found a gunny bag and lured Mishka into it, then stitched up the head of the bag and threw it into the tennis court. All night Mishka screeched and yowled for deliverance. Dona Rosa could hear her cries for help, and she sent Wolcott out to search for her. It was dark in the tennis court, and the gunny-bag was a moving prison of pain and bewilderment. But cat spirits are strong and indomitable, and just before dawn Mishka managed to break loose.

The violent movements that preceded her release had managed to terrify an old porcupine that was resting in a patch of grass and dandelion by the edge of the tennis court. I have observed that fear and pain are inextricably linked in your dimension. The startled porcupine let loose a volley of quills, and poor Mishka was stabbed by an arrow of poison. The porcupine scampered back into the woods, and Mishka confronted the new terror and affliction. She did not understand what had happened, what events and forces had conspired to hurt her so – she knew only that her deliverance lay with Dona Rosa. She returned to the house. The journey was an exercise in faith and courage. It was the staircase that was the most difficult, each step involving a piercing reinforcement of her suffering as the quill wobbled deeper into the wounded flesh.

It was only the next morning that Dona Rosa discovered that Mishka had returned. The piteous heap of fur moved her kind heart to an instant outburst of tears. The porcupine quill was still embedded firmly in Mishka's neck, and she froze stock-still upon Dona Rosa's approach, on no account allowing herself to be touched. A cornered cat is an angry and desperate sight. Dona Rosa sighed and left a saucer of milk behind the curtain, which Mishka lapped up hungrily.

I studied Mishka during the time that she hid behind the curtain with me. It was not thought that drove her; I could sense the intense urgency of communication from her mid-brain as she crouched and hid like a penitent fugitive. Every time Dona Rosa approached, her blood pressure would rise and her blood vessels dilate. She would hiss and growl, and her back and tail hair would stand on end, erect as the porcupine quill that had pierced the soft black fur of her neck. A quill, as I understand it, is itself an extreme form of armoured hair, a device of both warning and protection.

For thirteen days Mishka hid behind my curtain, ears pressed back, teeth bared, a mass of nervous electrical energies, a study in forbearance, stubbornly waiting for the agony to abate, which in time it did. The quill fell out and the hurt eased and the warm milk and Dona Rosa's love gave her new strength and sustenance. Mishka would now sit on Donna Rosa's lap and purr, even though her neck had not yet healed. A cat-purr is a sound of perfect contentment, its resonance carries a balance of activity and rest, of watching and waiting. Once she was well Mishka left the house for ever, for cats are quick to learn from misery and wise enough to keep away from it.

It is at this juncture of my story that the most magical moment in my dismal continuum is placed. I can recall it all so clearly – the sense of lightness, of glory, of pure joy, that accompanied my love.

I remember observing her one evening, as she sat by the window, watching the darkness set in and the stars arrive. Her eyes were troubled by some emotion I could not decipher. She was weeping, tears were streaming down her cheeks, she was licking them as they reached her mouth, she was sniffling slightly, her being was textured with the essence of salt. There was sweat in the slightly matted hair of her underarms, and below, in the warm moist void between her legs, there was a hunger which frightened me: I sensed then what it must be like to be a man, to be beckoned and drawn there, to be summoned, to surrender one's store of the vital force in a sticky mess of sad delight.

I searched into her belly, her soft, swelling belly, and then I looked deep into her essence, as she sat profiled in the brooding shadows before the dying fire. I saw her in a mist of erotic enchantment. She was wearing nothing but a Spanish shawl. I could glimpse the tangle of fur-like hair, sense the heat emanating from her core. Within her womb I saw that a seed had come to life. It was my seed, it bore the imprint of my being. I felt a sense of renewal, a binding to the life process, an acceleration of the continuum. Needless to say, I had never felt these things before.

Magic is mutability, it is change, it is an understanding and control of the will of the universe. The magic of human creation had propelled my seed into her womb, that night when I had offered her the homage of the fireflies. By the paradox of creation, by fusion and fission, the crawling sperm that Wolcott and I had let loose within her sat triumphant in her womb, a little foetus feeding, fattening, feasting on my love.

I had rent the shroud of non-being that had been my fate. There was no option for me now, no choice but that I take form and become immanent. I regretted that there was no better vehicle for my materialisation than that worm Wolcott, but then linear time is full of these travesties, these inescapable incongruities. So it is with the egg of the cuckoo, so it was with the Immaculate Conception.

Wolcott chose that precise moment to return to the room, murmuring some mumbo-jumbo which he had doubtless picked up in an encyclopaedia of magic. 'Under this Night of Pan I come to worship the womb of our Lady Babylon, impregnated with the egg of life!' he said, in the sibilant whisper that never failed to infuriate me. 'She changes everything she touches – and everything she touches, changes . . .' Even as he crossed the threshold of the door I mounted him. He did not notice or suspect my entry, for he was not at all a sensitive man, and after a brief struggle with his psyche I was again completely in command. Dona Rosa was more perceptive, and as she turned to look at me I sensed again that empathy, that understanding with which she had met my embraces the first time I made love to her.

I had entered Wolcott brutally; I knew already that when I finally left him he would be in no position to survive. Yet leave him I must: it was only will that had propelled me, and I could not fuel this metamorphosis for ever. There is a stage at which we become the possessions of those we possess.

Abandon is at the heart of change. Imago, pupa, chrysalis – all are process, all phases of becoming. Wolcott, in spite of his pretensions, was no magician. He stuck to his past, to his succession of selves, with a sense of stubborn reluctance. He could not even let go of old love-letters when the need arose. A magician has to be in love with change, and therein Dona Rosa was a better practitioner of the craft. She had slain, buried, slipped out of, outwitted, so many of her past personas that she had become an adept. And yet, somewhere at her centre, she had retained a pure motionless stillness.

I am beginning to display the sentimentality so fatal to lovers. Love, like magic, is an illusion, but at least it is that. Reality is a shoddy hoax. When, like us, you can see the spaces between things, the inconsequences between actions and events, the human belief in reality is at best laughable.

Reality is an imposed superstructure, a construct of the internal imagination as defined by immediate circumstance. For me it was an alien paradox which I had to carefully and respectfully circumvent. Yet I discovered that both Dona Rosa and Wolcott surrendered to its tyranny with a subservience quite at odds with their enthusiasm for the occult and the magical. Reality is uncharted territory – humans placate it quite differently than for example my friends the crows. KailKaran and his lot assign and confront a world quite similar to the human – yet the crow-mind has a capacity infinitely superior to the human in understanding. And then, even in human terms, Dona Rosa was silly. Silly but beautiful.

We who stay close to the incandescent emptiness understand

unreality but I confess that fitting snug as a glove into Wolcott's well-hung corporeality altered my mode of perception. Everything became immediate. The sequencing between the past, present and future whispered always to the next: the next moment, the next kiss, the next meal. Although I had supplanted Wolcott in his body, effected a coup, as it were, still his habits and instincts and intuitions remained his. I was in equal danger of being annihilated by the triviality of his daily life.

Life as humans live it has a pattern that is quite tedious. They falter in their dreams, awake, defecate the wastes from their bodies, engorge some food (hot liquids in the mornings) – then they fritter away their days in a series of unnecessary and uncoordinated movements towards some elusive and imaginary goals. Tired, they engorge themselves again and then attempt to capture and penetrate each other in a simulation of passion. Then a return to the rhythm of sleep, and dreams that are not dreams but the clutter and refuse of unassimilated daytime images. What was I doing in such a world?

All these discomforts, the pinchings of the shoe, were amply compensated by the proximity of my beloved Dona Rosa, she who bore my seed. Yet, with human eyes, I began to notice the presence of imperfections and even defects in this incomparable woman. She had, for example, a long bristly hair that protruded from her left nostril, like the antenna of a beetle. Her eyes crinkled up a little too much when she was thoughtful or amused, and the texture of her eyelids was not youthful. Her breasts sagged, you could even call them flaccid, and her breath stank.

Father Benedictus once explained to me that beauty was merely a form of intelligence. There were times when Dona Rosa was not beautiful – when her will collapsed, when her smile fluttered uncertainly on her bared lips, when her eyes were greedy with the insecurity of desire. But these fluctuations were on the whole rare, for Dona Rosa's extraordinary generosity of spirit mirrored some deeper secrets of the human universe.

I still loved her, the essence of her, the pulsating energy I had seen from the other world, but I realised that her lover Wolcott did not entirely share my feelings. Sometimes I even tended to agree with him. The human body is, all said and done, a gross and ineffectual machine. The process of incorporating and excreting food, fuelling and evacuating the organs, has always struck me as plainly repulsive. When, at the dinner table, I would watch Dona Rosa wipe a morsel of bread from her lips, or chew ruminatively on a tough piece of meat (for the meat in that house was always tough) I would experience the most intense alienation from my circumstances, and yearn for the formless grace of my essential self.

I was already beginning to chafe under the restraints of a human body; my existence by proxy was beginning to pall. The continuous and enforced contiguity to Captain Wolcott was proving hateful. I could hear the constant and ceaseless cycle of his breathing, in–out, inhale–exhale, and the sheer monotony and repetitiveness of this pattern drove me to the brink of mutiny. The cilia in his nostrils swaying when he sneezed, the gurglings of his duodenum, the complaints and intrigues and aggravations amongst the colonies of friendly bacteria that populated the busy interstices of his body, the morose whinings of the worms that inhabited his intestines – the physicality of it all sickened me. I found it unpleasant in the extreme, and I longed to return to a disembodied state.

Not having a body, I found it most difficult to come to terms with the problems of pain. Picture Wolcott with a stomach ache:

he had a weak digestion, besides which he tended to overeat because of the worms. As I inhabited his body, I inhabited his pain. When his stomach hurt he devolved into a quaking mass of tissue, his already restricted and enclosed consciousness further withdrawing into itself in a spasm of fear, becoming naught but the contractions of his abdomen.

I understood then that the ultimate measure of your reality is the degree of pain and resistance which the environment offers to the nervous system. For the human race, the body above all is the instrument of suffering.

But it was worth it, it was all worth it, for that rush of blood and that change of body and contour, that uncoiling serpent of manhood, and then the gropings of the body, the dancing of the pelvis, as our souls searched in each other's eyes for any signs of recognition.

I loved Dona Rosa more dearly than ever before, the intimacy of human life made me see and realise and sense and feel her charms in dimensions I could never have dreamt of before. She had a way of waking up in the mornings and looking around her in a puzzled, perplexed manner, as though she had just awoken for the very first time in her life. She did this every morning without fail, and I found the entire ritual of her rubbing her eyes and her subsequent wide-eyed wonder at her surroundings heart-stoppingly and achingly beautiful.

When the birdsong reverberates through the hills, when the gauzy spider webs, labours of the night, are lit up by the first rays of white-tinged dawn – it is at this time that the tangled web of dreams, the ragtag of memory and desire, makes room for the clear pure perceptions of the roaming psyche, let free for a while from its bodily trap to pursue its own shadows in the hunting grounds of time. It is at this point in the trajectory of the day that the past and the future furl and unfurl in the eternal present.

Early in the morning, as I stepped into Dona Rosa's dreaming mind, I encountered there a passage from Aeschylus (a passage which my beloved had never read, I can vouch for that) – where he says of Helen, she of Troy – 'Soul as serene as the calm of the seas, beauty that adorns the richest finery, gentle eyes piercing like an arrow, flower of love fatal to hearts.' Somewhere betwixt the worlds his shadow had encountered the wandering reveries of Dona Rosa, of my Laura, and recognised therein the becalmed eternity where such creatures rule and destroy their subjects. Perhaps, after all, she had not been wrong, it was not vanity alone which led her to remember Clytemnestra and Nemesis, perhaps it was the sad seamstress who was the aberration in her succession of selves. And then I saw the sea, the blue Mediterranean sea, and Laura, somebody who could have been or might some day be Laura, holding a seashell in her soft outstretched hands and examining it with wonder.

Wolcott of course slept through it all, inhale–exhale inhale–exhale with his heavy bloated sleepers' breathing. She would wake up at the very crack of dawn and examine the world around her with the candour and curiosity of a child, and then, still looking a little puzzled, her eyes still crinkled, her face a little crumpled, return to her dreams. It became my habit to enter her mind at this time, and always, in the mornings, she would dream of water – of Aphrodite rising from the waves, the blue breaking of the sea on a sandy shore, of the sea-serpent's eyes as it examined a drowning shape.

One morning, as our uneasy *ménage à trois* was facing the new day with varying degrees of composure, a guest arrived from the outside world. A young German stood at the front door, dishevelled and bedraggled after the long journey from the plains. He was escorted by two native hill men who had taken upon themselves the task of escorting the stranger to the big house. Even as the shadows of war hung over their continent, this young man sought refuge from his fears by travelling to distant lands. What he sought was of course an illusion, the wishful culmination of his fears, and his retreat led him to this mistaken asylum.

Nicholas Mann – that was his name – had been sent by his guru to seek instruction from the Himalayan Masters. He was accompanied by his friends, a German man and an Indian woman, who were parked at the local dak bungalow while he sought the way. It was a case of inspired confusion, for the quartet of seekers had been despatched by this guru to an ashram near Almora, and their party was more than eighty miles off course from their intended destination. But when Wolcott, that incurable romantic, heard that the third of the party was an Indian princess, his constant and unremitting desire for the exotic triumphed over his already defeated scruples. He rendered the German an effusive welcome, kissing him upon both cheeks, according him a series of hugs and kisses and then, allowing him no ground for retreat, leading him by the arm to the vacant guest room upstairs.

His Pahari escorts were sent to bring back the remaining members of the party. The hill men left as phlegmatically as they had come, their shrewd brown eyes lighting up only at the sight of the rupee coins that Captain Wolcott gave them to speed them on their mission.

The servants began cleaning in an atmosphere of bustle and confusion. Marcus's old room was made ready for the Princess, and fresh linen was taken out from the musty cupboard by the landing and aired in the bright summer sunshine. A wasps' nest was discovered by the window, and hastily smoked out. My beloved Dona changed into her favourite blue frock, and got out a string of pearls from her jewellery case, and matching earrings. After consultation with the mirror she took them off again, replacing them with an Egyptian set of gold and lapis lazuli, and earrings fashioned like scarabs.

Dona Rosa was so excited at the prospect of company that she rushed to the garden and busied herself gathering an enormous bouquet of flowers for the Princess's room. She held them to her face and smelt them: the tender young sweet-peas that were just beginning to blossom on the bamboo trellis, the last of the radiant primrose which grew by the bamboo clump as one entered the house, the pale purple hydrangea from the enormous bush by the rosebeds, and then larkspur and lupins and of course the red and white roses that flowered in such joyous profusion near the veranda. She was happy as she gathered the flowers, her strong white teeth were bared in a carefree smile, and she hummed and whistled and even broke into a merry dance as she ran about the fragrant garden.

I confess that I was uneasy about the unexpected arrival of these strangers. Six is a magical number, it creates new and unexpected resonances. The power of six, its vibrancy, was further compounded by the circumstance that I, the sixth among them, was not even visible or attenuated to the others. I knew, I sensed, that their coming would interrupt the equilibrium I had so tenuously maintained within the unlikely troika of my beloved and my host her lover.

Nicolas Krutz, the second of the Germans, entered the garden, past the outhouse and the clump of bamboo that framed the triangular snow peak of Nanda Devi. Even as he was recovering from the startling beauty of that sight, from the unreal impact of dazzling snow and blue sky and the clear mountain air that so heightens the senses, he saw Dona Rosa in her blue frock, her slender neck encircled with scarabs, the immense bunch of sweet-peas and primrose and hydrangea and lupins and larkspur and white and red roses in her arms, and an infatuated bee buzzing around her bosom. At that moment Nicholas Mann came down from his bedroom, past the veranda into the garden. Instantly and simultaneously they fell in love with her, both of them. The love swelled and rose within their bodies like a poem or a prayer, they were speechless and silent and in danger of dying from the sheer weight of their happiness at the sight of her as she stood before them, the flowers in her arms. Perhaps it was the flowers that did it, the colours and fragrances and energies they released as they nestled near her heart. Or perhaps it was just because she was so lovely.

They shared the same name, Nicolas Krutz and Nicholas Mann, but they were in retreat from different things: they were running away from different fears, they were fleeing from their pasts, but although they could run from their homes they could not run from their hearts. Nicolas Krutz was stalked by a nameless guilt that overcame him in the most far and distant and secret places, that was why he had sought the Himalayan Master, and suddenly, in a summer garden where the breeze ruffled his ears and played with his collar his heart was unburdened of the inexplicable weight which had carried him here, so far from where he had once begun.

Nicholas Mann was a voyager, a journeyer, a man impelled by the nature of his being to seek that which he could not easily find, and upon finding it always to leave it behind. When he saw my beloved he knew that this search had come to an end, that he had finally found what he was questing; he knew the moment he saw her that now he could rest for ever. I recognised their emotions, and I did not feel jealous, for I shared with them the celebration of her beauty and was grateful for their homage.

Dona Rosa introduced herself and led them up the stairs to their bedrooms, the two Germans and the lady who was with them, the Indian princess we had all forgotten. Only she was neither Indian nor a princess. Veera was an Armenian from Calcutta whose sister was the mistress of a famous ruler from Rajasthan; her sister lived in a flat in Bombay with this prince, surrounded by solitaires and Siamese cats. Unfortunately one cannot enter laterally into a royal bloodline, but Veera was trying anyway, while simultaneously pursuing the salvation of her soul. She was delighted by the flowers, and flattered by Dona Rosa's affectionate welcome, but it was when Captain Wolcott sauntered into the room, surrounded by the invisible cloud of stupidity and heat that made him irresistible to women, that her heart and certain other parts of her anatomy were enflamed by love and, burning with an intensity that resisted flames, released themselves to him in a heap of ashes.

It is an irony of the human condition that in the course of their short and tedious passage through the closed corridors of time, humans truly live but a few hours of their lives. Trapped in that summer day, in the sticky heat and the blue sky, was the most intense spectrum of emotions that the three of them, Nicolas and Nicholas and the brave Veera, were ever to experience in their brief existences. Dona Rosa and mine host Wolcott, the objects of these new and intrepid loves that fluttered into their lives like leaves buffeted by the breeze, were completely unaware of and unconcerned about the ravage and ruination that had already been set in motion in the deceptive calm of that balmy summer morning. They were not to be spared the consequences of that fatal human sickness, that malady without repair which your race calls love. The fever rose in their blood like a tide, encircling their auras, enlivening their motions, rendering their tired eyes incandescent and gay. As they settled down for a light repast in the dining room downstairs where Mrs Cockerell's pathetic watercolours were smeared upon peeling walls, and rice and curry and potatoes were served by languid servants, as the wine which Wolcott had sacrificed from his dwindling stock stained the white tablecloth with spatters and circlets of crimson, as the wine warmed their throats and the warmth travelled down their bodies to their guts and then further, a madness was released into the air.

It was a madness compounded of many things: of the spent furies of the strange passions that had roamed this house, of the summer solstice whose day it was, of the sudden loves that had assaulted them and left them bereft of the usual solace and comfort of their incomplete selves, and most of all of the absurd prank which the servants had played upon their masters by lacing the curry with vast quantities of hashish. It was that day the festival of Bikhauti, when 'Mesh', the constellation of the Ram, is celebrated in these hills, with betel leaves and sweetmeats, wine and *bhang*, song and merriment. The local *bhang*, the dream-weed marijuana had surrendered its magical potencies at the grinding-stone in the kitchen, and the madness it bred lurked in every morsel of food the sahibs swallowed.

Their conversation at the dinner table was innocuous: they

talked of the weather and of the hot spices, which they all except Veera relished, and of the strange and incongruous circumstances which had brought them together on this midsummer's day, perhaps by fate, perhaps by accident. Yet strange emanations of sexuality and desire, of bodily appetite and biological urge, of flesh and prurience, of desire, itch and carnal passion, crowded the closed air of the dining room.

Veera talked of her sister's flat in Bombay, which she described as her own. Her recitation of her wealth only fanned Wolcott's lusts, thereby disturbing and disconcerting me, for I couldn't tolerate her, I found her large teeth and her vapid stare repugnant. I shrivelled back into that white cold void, driven away by Wolcott's proximity to her as he bent over to gaily whisper something in her ear, his hand brushing against her breast with an elaborate show of accident.

'Do what thou wilt, that is the Whole of the Law.' Those were the words that Wolcott whispered into Veera's ear, her ear with the thumb-sized diamond dangling from it, which she had borrowed from her sister in Bombay. 'Love is the Law! That is the wisdom my master has taught me!' Wolcott continued fervently, biting and nibbling gently at her ear, licking the diamond as he spoke, as he began telling her of the revels at Boleskine, of the mysteries of Bacchus and of lusts sacred and profane.

Wolcott's loins were afire with purpose. In his imagination he could already see himself in a maharaja's harem, a jewelled turban upon his handsome forehead, adorned with a peacock feather, perhaps – rubies and emeralds around him in great profusion, lying like bunches of grapes upon silver bowls, while nubile women ministered to his every need. As he awoke from his daydream and examined the dish of sliced mangoes the servant had placed before him, and saw the reflection from the hard glittering light of the diamonds that dangled from Veera's ears, he resolved at that moment to marry her.

Nicolas, Nicolas Krutz that is, was in the meanwhile swooning from the weight and burden of his desire, his organ was almost insensate with lust. His pink tongue was heavy with uncommunicated kisses and the sweet taste of mangoes, and he felt as though he might actually burst. Sugar serves to intensify the hallucinatory properties of hashish, and the mountain of mangoes that Nicolas was devouring released dreams and demons within him he had never dared to recognise. Dona Rosa's mouth, that pink rosebud from which petals of laughter were scattering, the sides of which were sticky with mango, giving it the look of a blush rose – Nicolas Krutz reached out across the dining table to Dona Rosa's mouth and gave her a resolute kiss.

No one was in the least surprised by this behaviour, although I squirmed with anger and exasperation as I watched from my perch near Wolcott's heart, where my sensibilities were still recoiling from that woman Veera. The hashish had not worked upon her, but she adored Wolcott anyway. She was giving him the benefit of a feline sort of rub, her body was crawling against his in a way that to her mind signified sexuality.

I cursed myself for my stupidity and wished that I had possessed the foresight to penetrate the new contender for my beloved's charms. But it was too late already. Dona Rosa's self-love had been actuated by his adoration; she was looking at Nicolas Krutz with rapture. Her eyes were sparkling with the brilliance that rightfully belonged to the rocks attached to Veera's earlobes, and her lips were moist, stained crimson from the wine and a deep wanton golden from the mangoes. The smell of mangoes clung to her like an aphrodisiac, a smell compounded of summer afternoons and the sated sensuality of that fecund fruit.

Nicholas Mann, who had observed the other Nicolas kiss Dona Rosa, who had watched helplessly as he observed the sparkle in her eyes and the invitation in her lips, was feeling miserable. The hashish had activated in him a grand and thunderous grief, a storm of feelings had encircled him, he knew this perfect summer day would not last and that tears followed laughter: that was what had been taught to him as a child by his grandmother in Düsseldorf. He felt like abandoning himself to laughter or to weeping, or perhaps both. As I observed his predicament, as I watched his pain with a sympathy born of understanding, I could not really tell if he was surrendering to a black merriment at the irony of this sudden love or, with the forward vision of the strong man, was already grieving over his joy.

The cloying smell of sweet over-ripe mangoes had filled the room. As we walked out into the afternoon sun the light hit us like a hammer, and the blinding white of the Himalayan snows assailed us, making me cringe and long for the shy comforting shadows of the dark dining room. It is unusual to glimpse the snows on a summer afternoon, they are hidden by a pall of heat and dust, but nothing about that afternoon followed the norm of what is usual. Our eyes adjusted to the brilliant sun and we surrendered to the beauty of the day. As the human eye has an aperture that adjusts itself to the degree of light around it, so it is with the human heart, and Nicholas Mann had already reconciled his heart to the pain Dona Rosa was bound to offer it. As for me, it was only after being accommodated for so long in Captain Wolcott's human frame that I could venture out in the bright light of day.

There is a stream that flows by a field a little way from the house – that same stream by whose waters the girl Fanny had read poetry and swooned in her sad hopes and expectations. As we walked there, past the fragrant garden, past the tennis field so quiet now, so calm, our senses were assaulted by a succession of smells. There were the flavours of the earth, of mud and soil and pebbled shelter, the dry grass that shrank and shrivelled at our arrival, the dank secrets of decay and renewal that festered in the armpits of the hills where the path turned and curved. And then the smells of honeysuckle and apple-blossom, of ripe red plum whose oozing juices dripped to the ground and stained and bloodied it, and the sharp bitter smell of pine-needles, of the watchful pine trees with their dry cracked bark and their crooked spines and cackling laughter which no one but I could hear.

We were in a meadow full of flowers, where scattered sunlight dappled the undulating swell of white and yellow narcissus. It smelt like paradise. Wolcott took a deep long breath, and a change overcame him, something pure and noble entered him, a sense of abandon overtook him. He forgot for the moment about Veera and her diamonds and her flat in Bombay which overlooked the blue waters of the Arabian sea, he forgot the anxieties about unpaid bills and creditors and the sad reminders of fidelity from his mother and sister and so many others; he remembered only an afternoon in Boleskine when the Master Thereon had initiated him in the art of forgetting.

A stream babbled in the background. Its waters were pure and clean. It was fed by a spring that crept like a cautious thief from the ridge of the hill. Green moss and clumps of ferns clustered and sheltered by its banks. The hot summer had already exerted its tyranny over the landscape, but this spot offered a promise of reprieve – there was something in it that was good, benign and protected. I felt a flutter of wings, and even with the human eyes that were Wolcott's I saw the shape of an angel, a winged, luminous form. It hovered briefly before us and then with a smile that was both sad and forgiving it departed.

'Everything that is, is right . . .' Wolcott whispered. He was speaking the words to no one but himself. He smiled at Dona Rosa as he spoke; there was a radiance and effulgence about him that led the others, Nicolas and Nicholas, and Veera, to draw back from the charged circle of our love. And there in that field of flowers he entered her, he lifted up her blue dress and gently swathed his body in hers. There was joy and triumph and damnation and hell in our union, our bodies shook and shuddered as we watched the blue sky with the keeling hawks, the kites that rode the air and watched us from above, and around us the turning earth where we did not any longer belong.

Where the stream fell and met its sister in the next hill, at that spot somebody (the girl Fanny, perhaps) had planted an arbour of vine trees. Veera had wandered off in a state of trancelike exultation, she walked among the flowers and drank in their keen fragrance, she tossed off her shoes and felt the moist earth between her toes. A ladybird settled upon her arm and she watched it navigate through the jungle of fine brown down and the golden arch of her bangle to the painted crimson islands of her fingernails. She experienced an immense sense of freedom, of surrender and quietude. Contrary to popular imagination, nature rarely nurtures humans. There is usually a hostile tilt to the balance. On that midsummer day some random grace, some passing benediction was granted to that bunch of mortals and the lost spirit that was me. The afternoon lasted for ever, it escaped the confines of time and stretched into an eternity of virginal and elastic plenitude.

Wolcott held Laura's urging breasts to his mouth and fell asleep in their embrace.

Veera approached him with love written upon her countenance, which was at that moment awkward and expectant and surprisingly beautiful. In her hands, which the ladybird was still busily exploring, she held a wreath of vine-leaves which she gently draped around Wolcott's face. Dona Rosa got up, she buttoned up her bodice and walked away. Wolcott awoke, his forehead wreathed with vine-tendrils, the broad leaves clustered around his brow; there was a laughter in his eyes I had never known before. He straddled Veera there among the flowers, and underneath those leaves I discovered his horns.

Dona Rosa was naked, and although her face was vulnerable her soft body had the musculature and taut strength of an athlete. She took on Nicholas Mann, she invited him with a smile and a nod, she ripped off his shirt in a fury of passion; her body as she took him to her was humid as a plant, her saliva was warm and salty on his parched lips, her hands felt through his body as though in search of something, something he did not possess. I knew this because I was there with him, in this place where I belonged, in the long silence where the only sounds were the successive waves of our seeking.

Krutz patiently awaited his turn, but it was not to be. By the end of these couplings they were all absolved of sin, they were all children again, and when Laura kissed Krutz it was with the timid touch of a little girl. Satiated, they had forgotten the hungers of the body, and a larger joy had flooded their consciousness. Their fears and guilts were appeased and forgiven, they were by now all very tired, and suddenly, after an eternity, the sun was ready to set and time resume its course.

Nicolas Krutz was disconsolate. He lit a cigarette and sat alone and sulked as the others walked back to the house, hand in hand through the fields. The golden mountains glittered in the sunset, and then there was only the wan shadow of the snows as the sky and earth turned dark, and dark the gurgling stream and dark the silent forest which awoke only at night when the eyes of prowlers and predators signalled danger and challenge through the sleeping presences of the trees.

Krutz remained rooted to his spot beside the stream, he looked at the inky twilight that filtered through the sky and floated amongst the fields of narcissus, which yielded even more intoxication as the night progressed. He watched the constellations crowd the night sky; the Great Bear stretched like a huge suspended question mark, pointing its way to the true north. The night fragrances disquieted him: they would alternately lull and excite, and he felt alone and shunned and condemned to solitude. He smoked cigarette after cigarette, and the red glow from his mouth puzzled and frightened the animals who were not used to human presences. There was only a small hare which was not afraid: it ventured out from the forest and stood and stared at Krutz from across the stream, its delicate nose picking up the separate and disparate smells which surrounded him, its pink eyes following the wisps of smoke that rose from the burning tobacco.

In the deodar tree, my friend the crow KailKaran was dying. His spirit was slipping away from his crow-body. He looked already like a taxidermist's toy. His coat had lost its lustre, and his wise beady eyes were focused inwards in the deepest meditation. His neck was bent forward, as though he was listening intently to something nobody else could hear. He had been motionless in that very position for two days now, but he had been alive. Yet when he switched dimensions, although there was no discernible change in his posture or anything like that, all the other crows of the seven surrounding mountains knew that his time had come. They flew forth to salute him, and set up such a collective wailing that their grief could be heard for miles around.

The servants heard it in the quarters of the old house and looked anxious, for as an omen it was not good. My lady of the deodar tree, in whose bosom these lamentations had been let loose, shed a few tears herself. Her tears settled upon the trunk of the tree, on the brown and grey bark. They looked like turpentine, or gum arabic, but they were born of grief. KailKaran had been the *vanbhanjika's* friend for many years now. She had been his confidante, and he never failed to amuse her with his sarcasm and his subtle sense of humour.

KailKaran's uncle, much older than him in years but destined to watch and listen to the world for many more, initiated the formal ceremonies of mourning. The crows came forward, in their designated order of seniority, and bent their black necks before KailKaran's rigid form, lifting up their claws slightly to signify respect. Then, one by one, in sequence and hierarchy, they each tugged and pulled a feather from his wing and held it in their beaks. When he was completely shorn of all but the black down on his chest and sternum, six young crows, who had stood apart and waited for the de-feathering ceremony to be completed, filed up before him and held him between their beaks.

The crows set off, their wings scarcely flapping, in keeping with the intense dignity of the occasion. They flew in the dark towards the peak of Kabbalekh, near Danpur, to the west of Nanda Devi, where the twice-born crows are interred. When a crow is on the point of death he goes to Kabbalekh. If a crow dies elsewhere, another crow takes a feather from its wing and drops it over Kabbalekh.

The villagers, already at their tasks at the crack of dawn, saw them, gliding and soaring in perfect formation in the sky above, and they lowered their eyes, for they knew with the wisdom of peasant folk that some things are not to be seen. After they had completed their task, the crows scattered and flew off in different directions, shaking and flapping their wings so that the spirits of Kabbalekh could not pursue them as they returned to the world that clings to the surface of the earth.

It was the native festival of Bikhauti, the sign of the Ram was at the zenith. That night, the god Pan, of winged foot and fickle fancy, Pan the friend of Wolcott's mentor Aleister Crowley, roamed and wandered the corners of the old house, singing and shouting his laughter. Through the murky mists of Wolcott's memory, the mischievous song echoed the corridors of the house and its draughty chimneys, across the solid and ethereal manifestations of mind and matter, this song which the wind whistled, the night sang, the darkness lisped.

Come, O come!
I am numb
Manikin, maiden, maenad, man,
In the night of Pan
Io Pan! Io Pan Pan! Pan! Io Pan!

New lusts arose from the slumbering forms of the tired revellers, and dissipation and licentiousness were palpable presences, flesh-and-blood personifications that reached out to tease and provoke those four mortals to test the limits of their mortality. My Donna, my noble Laura, my pure and sacred flame of life, became but a slut and a slattern; Veera, who had never known a shard of honour, reverted to her normal nature of bitch and strumpet. As for the men, they were enflamed by hungers they had never imagined and could not slake. Debauchery and perversity are but the tired rituals of sensual gratification. Delivered from reason, liberated from dignity, they became participants in a greater hungering, a collective yearning for what they could never have. Their fevered bodies searched and writhed in vain, they danced the old dance with new and jaded steps. Outside, the ancient night greeted the return of the equinox, and celebrated the balance of the worlds.

Nicolas Krutz sat alone in the dark forest. He felt a sense of abandonment, of alienation, which he knew and recognised from his early childhood. He was also very hungry, his stomach was literally growling with hunger. He lit a cigarette and looked up at the black sky: it had a darkness different from the one he knew and associated with night.

'This is a jungle, not a forest,' he said aloud to himself, and suddenly everything seemed to fall into place. It was as though the categorisation had released a deeper understanding about the nature of things, of forests and jungles and darkness and solitude. He thought of Dona Rosa, as she had stood in the garden of the old house, a bunch of flowers in her arms, and an electric seizure of desire ran through his body until he actually felt as through his entire nervous system was on fire. 'So that is what love is . . .' he said to himself, savouring the words as he said them. The words did not seem to penetrate the night. They bounced up a few feet and floated above him in the dense air, which was thick with the smells of the forest, with night flowers and civet smells and the heady overpowering fragrance of the narcissus.

A pair of striped grey and black marmots, the Himalayan *chitrail* that our hill people consider so extremely unlucky, ventured cautiously out of the tree cover into the field and stood and stared in awe and wonder at the golden eye of the cigarette, sniffing all the while to determine the nature of the smoke that floated above Krutz's reclining body. 'Now I know what love is,' Krutz said aloud again, '. . . now I am finally ready to die.'

The marmots began decimating the flowers, uprooting the bulbs and nibbling at them with ferocious speed. Suddenly their ears peaked up and their eyes met. An instinct too deep for fear had alerted them to an ancient enemy. They knew the soft pad of tiger paws, too soft to be heard; they smelt the raw and bloody breath of the predator. Abandoning the tender bulbs, they sped away in one clear long motion, leaving only a flattened patch of flowers behind them.

Krutz was still lost in his thoughts. The entire course of the day replayed itself in his mind with painful clarity. He saw it all again and again – Dona Rosa in the garden, the kiss he had given her in the dining room, the soft pressure of her lips as she responded, the taste of mangoes in her mouth, the wine and curry on her breath. And then he remembered the afternoon as it had progressed: Wolcott, Dona Rosa, Nicholas Mann, the connections between them, the abandonment, the freedom, the joy! It was as though he was possessed by them, he became a participant in their mysteries, summoning up the spirits that had so possessed them.

He could hear the busy night sounds of the forest, of twigs

snapping and the soft rustle of undergrowth. He got to his feet, but the cannabis-induced expansion of consciousness had left him strangely limp. A cloud of fireflies approached; it was as though the night stars had descended into the field. They fluttered around him, each point of light stabbing his eyes with unexpected intensity.

Krutz felt as though he had wandered into a fairy tale, that he was under the spell of some unknown enchantment, and that when he awoke he would be rewarded with some magical gift, a golden apple, perhaps.

In the distance he could hear the sad and insistent baying of dogs, a long, melancholy sound, *sau, sau, sau.* Then he saw before him a vision of two strange women. One had a stern, contorted expression, and the other wore a smile of ineffable joy and compassion. They were both wearing anklets that jingled as they walked, and the sound of their footsteps kept time with the baying of the dogs. Krutz could sense another presence as well, a masculine presence, but he could see no third person before him.

Joy and despair alternated in his heart like the polarities of some chemical experiment. The two women were dancing a peculiar dance around him, sometimes swaying, a-jitter, sometimes trembling. Krutz didn't know what to make of it – he stared at them as though paralysed. He felt as if they were sucking some strength from him, some sustenance, his life-force was being leeched out. His spirit sensed this, it screamed a silent protest, but his body was already ensorcelled, under their spell and power. There was a feeling of rapture, a feverish and frenzied sense of complete understanding, a glimpse of an elusive contiguous world, a world he was about to penetrate.

Krutz got to his feet and began dancing with them, in tune with their incantations. There was something familiar about the song, he knew he had heard it before. They danced together until he was exhausted, until he thought his limbs would fall off. The realities of his altered state registered themselves in flashes, in sharp images of unbearable intensity. He felt as though he were having a seizure. He noticed, in one of these snatches of vision, that the two women, the stern woman and the smiling one, both had feet that faced backwards.

'They pursue the past, not the future,' he thought to himself. Then he wasn't sure if it was he who had thought this, or if they had said it out loud to him. They continued with the dance, the backward-footed dance, and they lured him through it to some recess of exhausted, exhilarated consciousness and abandoned him there.

Where was he? Krutz knew with a sense of clarity and inevitability that he had reached a place of no return. He started running: he made a wild dash through the fields, through the dark-attenuated eyes of the blooming narcissus, through this field where others had fled before him. Overcome by the horror of it all, the terror, he plunged headlong into the dark reaches of the ravine, into the dark ravine further shadowed by the thick consciousness of the night.

In the ravine, the tiger waited patiently in the shadows for the moment when it must announce itself, the moment when it was ordained that it must strike and tear its prey apart.

Even as he fell, Krutz could still hear the distant baying of the dogs, and the weird laughter of the wood-witches followed him even as he leapt. His last thought, however, was of Dona Rosa and her laughing eyes, and the flowers she had held in her arms.

The stars glimmered and throbbed. Fleecy white clouds, herded together like docile sheep, shone in the luminous moonlight. In the north, flashes of lightning streaked the night sky. When the soul leaves its sheath the parting is never wrenching – it is a fluid, graceful transposition which is accompanied by an immense sense of freedom and forgetting. As the burden of the body is sloughed off, as the potential of new spaces and dimensions suddenly becomes apparent, the sounds of sorrowing farewell from the other side are dimmed, and the spirit progresses into its new and present state. But it was different for Krutz. As he died, as his soul left his body, that particulate mass of panic and regret, it was denied passage, it was seized and engorged by the presences that had hounded him to departure. He did not escape. A portion of him was to remain there, forever suspended, in that field beside the stream where the narcissus grew.

Krutz was dead. In the house, Nicholas Mann and Dona Rosa, Veera and Wolcott were still consumed by their madness, the perverse madness that had possessed them on this night of Pan, the madness of desire and satiety and cannabis-induced unreason.

I was in retreat from Wolcott, from Dona Rosa, from the others. I could at that moment say with perfect honesty and truth that everything human was repugnant to me. Marcus and Munro and the grand scales of their evil had left me unmoved, but the sexual greed, the devouring hunger of my pure and noble Laura sorrowed me beyond repair. There was no one and nothing she did not want; even the wanton Veera had to be tamed and subdued by her powers, her avaricious eyes had to bow in submission before Dona Rosa's rapacious appetite, her sleek body had to yield to the flagellant furies of my Helen's desires. These were needs I could not comprehend, they left in their wake a disturbed trail of formless despair, they repulsed and shamed me.

Why, I wondered, had I forgotten myself so far? It was too late now to turn and traverse a backward path – Wolcott and I had become totally enmeshed. We were both lost, only I knew it better than he. He was lost in his silly new infatuation with Veera and her diamonds. Laura moved him no longer, although the vortex of her lust aroused in him some small consternation. The marijuana was beginning to wear off, leaving in its stead a heavy sleep into which they all collapsed, one by one. They were lying naked and dishevelled before the fire, the four of them, Nicholas Mann, Veera, Wolcott and Dona Rosa. Nicholas Mann was asleep upon the chair, the same chair which had propelled Father Benedictus (blessed be his name) to the ceiling when he came to cleanse the house with his presence. Wolcott and Veera were entwined in each other's arms, the tufts of hair on their naked forms twisted and wet, their lips dry, their eyes blank. And Laura, my Dona, was curled up in an embryonic pose, her plump and pretty arm extending like an umbilicus towards the fire. Her brow was calm and her lips ruminative – her body had that peculiar stillness I associated only with her. In her belly the seed of our union slept expectantly. The fire gasped and guttered, and I knew with horror and regret exactly what I had to do. I had to control Wolcott, I had to steer him into the waiting arms of the fire, he had to die, we had both to die, before I could be reborn.

I could hear Wolcott snoring, that loud slow monotonous inhale–exhale I knew so well. Even as I re-entered him, entered the rhythm of his breathing, rolled and propelled his heavy form towards the amber eye of the fire, simultaneously I was busy stoking the passions of the flames, inciting them in turn to rush and spit at him, to slew out their anger, their devouring hatred. A fire is like a crowd: it has no barriers, it knows no boundaries, it wants to consume everything it encounters. Our dimension is familiar with this element, I knew already how the smouldering embers on the hearth could be transformed into spiteful vicious curls and tendrils of hungry flame. I knew exactly what to whisper to its incandescent heat so that it would become a hissing howling roaring force. Flame and fire, the smell of singed hair, flesh burning. Wolcott was no longer in Veera's arms, he was running and recoiling from the fire, he was reaching out in the moment of his departure for my beloved!

I realised just in time what was happening, and took my leave of the flames to return to ride Wolcott. His hair was on fire, his long golden mane of hair, and the tangled curls that sheltered around his penis. His heels were licked by flames of orange. Although the fire was hurting me, it was hurling me towards a luminescence of glowing pain, yet I had to save her. She could come to no harm. I entered the heart of the flame and led it by my volition out of the house. I did not permit Wolcott to roll down the stairs, to flatten himself against the floor, for that might have saved him; it was not entirely in his destiny to die. There was a portion of his fate that awaited a different outcome, but I allowed it no passage. I had to escape him; I had to destroy him.

Death by fire: it is an absolute condition. It was a glorious and beautiful sight, this human torch, those blazing brows, eyes blank with terror and knowledge. His hair shedding a million stars; it was a golden shower, the mane of a comet against the night sky. He ran, past the house, past the deodar tree, past the tennis court, until he reached the banks of narcissi where the stream bubbled and sang and the sated tiger burped in the shadows. He threw himself into the water, he quenched the fire, but it was too late. His skin had peeled off like the first layer of an onion, exposing the delicate tracery of capillary and vein. His eyebrows were charred into a look of exaggerated surprise. His face – his handsome well-proportioned face – was a pantomime mask of pain. Death by fire, death by water. As he yielded to the elements, Wolcott remembered the mysteries at Boleskine, and his master, the Great Beast Crowley.

The spirits of the three Sherpas looked on with deep satisfaction. The mountain snows of makalu still glimmered in their minds, and their anger, already dulled by time, was at last appeased. Crowley, too, was watching as his protégé made the passage to the next dimension. He found Wolcott's death distasteful, although he had for a moment admired the shower of sparks that fell from his long hair when, like a glittering arrow, he had rushed towards the stream.

Crowley had changed, he had at last grown up, he had stopped believing in magic. The great prankster had still not achieved wisdom (nor did he in any way aspire to it). He saw Wolcott's body floating in the stream, the water slowly bloating the same flesh the fire had just devoured. 'Silly fool,' he said to himself, and wandered off in search of another laugh.

For the fulfilled beast shall kick the consumed pail. There, finally, I allowed Wolcott to rest, and the smell of singed hair gave way to the bittersweet fragrance of charred narcissi, their tender green stems bending from the heat, collapsing back into the dry earth. In the east the dawn broke. Wolcott was dead, his spirit had departed in a haze of awful majesty. His guardian angel had not deserted him at the moment of his deepest betrayal, it had led him kindly by the hand from the blistering pain of extinguishment, and he was already somewhere else, safe, if a little bewildered.

As the morning broke over the Himalayas, the wan pale

presences of the mountains arose to the new day, turning amber and orange and a fluorescent pink. The sky became a fierce blue, and a white moon, a deformed scabrous hump, stood suspended like a blind witness to my crime. The dawn chorus broke into joyous song.

I could not face the day. Taking leave of my vanquished foe, I returned to the house. A glow brighter than the dawn accosted me. The deodar tree, the same gracious and noble tree which housed my beloved friend was on fire, its trunk bent against the anger of the conflagration. The colours of heat – orange, red, scarlet – leapt and danced around me. In the heart of the flames, centred in the blue licks, was a core of green, like the foliage of a peacock. Aphids and beetles and armies of ants retreated in panic from the blaze. The timid langurs had already fled. The crows, already sorrowing for KailKaran, quietly observed the destruction. In the heart of this busy spectacle the *vanbhanjika*, the dryad of the deodar, moaned and wept in helpless anguish. And then, even as the fire raged, she was still.

God knows I meant well!

Wolcott had won his revenge, his betrayal had been greater than mine. The fires I had instigated had infiltrated this most sacred and holy spot and made it profane with my follies. Grief was no remedy, sorrow no sop: there was no recall for my actions. At that moment I understood the nature of karma, but, as is usual in such cases, it was already too late.

Blinded by the light of the advancing day, I had no option but to retreat to the house. Even as I fled, the mighty edifice of their deodar tree tottered and stumbled and collapsed in a heap of twig and timber. It did not touch or hurt the house: it did not extend its anger; it did not aggravate the flames or incite them to further revenge, to more folly. The noble nature of the dryad, which I had long recognised and revered, asserted itself even in this moment of her destruction, and nothing and no one was hurt. The langurs, the wood beetles, the crows, all circled the once-mighty tree in circumspect grief and mourned the passing of that most noble spirit.

When Dona Rosa awoke, she felt calm and rested and content in a way she had never felt before. The life quickening in her belly had brightened her eye; her skin glowed unnaturally. Her breath was fresh and her movements were free. The excesses of the previous day had in no way disturbed the stillness of her deepest self. Her sleepy eyes examined her surroundings. Nicholas comatose on the chair, Veera snoring by the fireplace, her naked body sprawling in an unseemly mess. Her eyes registered these sights with faint surprise, and then she fell asleep again and dreamt of the windswept sails on the Aegean Sea.

I shall omit what happened next, for it is not a part of my story. I shall leave it to the reader to decipher: the disbelief, the confusion, the search for Nicolas Krutz, for Captain Wolcott. To add to the consternation, Veera's diamonds were lost, they had been stolen by one of the servants as she lay asleep before the fire. Already distraught by the loss she collapsed completely when Wolcott's body was discovered. As her hopes crumbled, her face became a pitiful swollen mass, her lips flaccid with defeat.

Dona Rosa had already decided to leave. She knew with her magician's sense of timing when departure was imminent. She instructed the servants to prepare her trunks, to line them with newspaper and mothballs, to fold and prepare her clothes, even as she took charge of the tragedy and converted it from chaos into internal order. The Colonel of the regiment was instructed to come and take possession of the remains of Wolcott's charred body. His letters, his pitiful lying stock of letters, were read and forgotten. His mother and sister were informed of his death. (They decided not to tell his abandoned wife, there was no point in it.)

The tombstone was ordered. Dona Rosa insisted that it was to have a carved angel on it. Even as the Colonel protested at the expense, and that a carved angel would have to be ordered all the way from Bareilly, and about the enormous cost of the conveyance, she gave him a smile of such transporting beauty that of course he had to succumb.

Veera was despatched back to Bombay, and although the regiment scoured the surrounding forests for Krutz's body, no such courtesies were extended for Veera's diamonds. Dona Rosa informed her coldly and with an air of contempt that they were just glass baubles her imagination had valued into diamonds. Didn't she feel she had caused enough trouble already in all their lives?

Father Benedictus once told me that every tragedy contained in its resolution a moral, and this was what made it a tragedy instead of the sorrowful mess which was life anyway. This tragedy, the sorrowful messy tragedy I had detonated, yielded its secret of strength and life to Nicholas Mann, he who had sat sleeping in the chair, dreaming of nothing, while I rolled poor Wolcott into the draughty fireplace. Nicholas awoke and reflected upon the strange events he had witnessed, and the spirit of Father Benedictus, which had conferred upon him the gift of deep understanding as he slept trustingly on the chair, guided and led him to the Himalayan Master who had summoned them to the mountains.

As for me, I returned to the ceaseless flow of the present, to my disturbed sleep and my furtive awakenings. My shame followed me like an accusing shadow for some time. But it was never in the nature of the lady of the deodar tree to cause pain, her spirit even in its departure could only soothe and heal and repair.

I contemplated the errors to which the human race (in which I had participated) were prone. The immutable laws of nature, if bent, cannot but rebound. Magic, like hope, is trivial and frivolous: it cannot understand or placate the fierce forces of the larger world. The redemption of your race lies in understanding the benign indifference of the universe, the amber heat of the tiger's eye, the blue depths of the mid-afternoon sky.

The brief conjunction of our lives had run its fated course. My beloved returned to Europe; she died at sea, with her unborn child. At the moment of her drowning, as the last gasp of air nourished her lungs, she reached out to me. Everything that had to be, had been. The past was over, the future was awaiting. Reality is the multiple unfolding of all possible events: in none of these was it ever posited that Dona Rosa would be mine.

Each of us is, ultimately, trapped in place or dimension, nobody is ever free. It was not to be. Even in death, in disembodiment, she was not to return to me, to my niche by this window, behind this curtain, to become mine. The mystery of love is that, knowing and understanding its impossibility, still the human soul exults in it. It is the first step in the ascending ladder of a larger mystery. But enough of big words and their betrayals, of the treachery taught to me by my friend Benedictus.

Sometimes, still, I yearn for her. The body flails and forgets, the heart remembers. I long for her, but although I can recall those days when I knew her, recollect their exact form and texture, I find

I cannot ever re-enter the unremitting stream of time. I saw her drown. I felt the water rush into her lungs, the blue water she had dreamt of, in the mornings when I had entered her, and then she awoke to another dream.

In the music it is the pauses that are important. Father Benedictus taught me that, stroking his white beard that flowed like a river, and then he played the music for me, without a piano, without a violin, without physicality, in his head. It was easier that way, for I do not of course possess any auditory receptors. He told me the names of great composers, which sadly I have forgotten, and explained the concept of the *mesure pour rien*, the bar's rest.

One cold winter night, as the snow fell softly on the garden outside the house, the bears come down from the forests and settled themselves on the veranda. There was no one in the house: it was between occupants. I love the house when it is left to itself, it falls into a dreaming and all the shades, present and future, dissolve into a silence as gentle as the falling snow outside. I can feel the frost from the window. Frost has an elegant and structured spirit, it cleanses and soothes the stale emotions, the high feelings, that sometimes I make this place so unruly.

I love the snow even more, it is so playful, it spars with the house, the trees, the wind. And here was a family of bears, Himalayan black bears with furry coats and snow on their snouts, sitting in our veranda, sheltering from the snow, looking at the white garden with patient eyes. The spirit of the bears is quite different from the spirit of the panthers, or of the playful malicious monkeys who rampage through the fruit trees in summer. They understand the earth, with which they are intimate, and to which they retreat every year for a renewal of their faculties. The bears are solitary souls, akin in their thought process to the human race. They think linear thoughts; they are not random in their consciousness. Further, they have a love for possessions quite unknown to the animal world. They want honey, they want pleasure, they lust for human women.

But these bears in the garden, of which one was a female, were not wanting or lusting for anything, they were only sheltering from the snow, for their cave in the higher reaches of the mountain had become inaccessible because of the bad weather.

I wondered at the difference between bears and humans, and tried to reach some conclusion on the subject. Bears are calm; although their acts are in accordance with both will and social sanction, yet they do not think, they do not attach image and meaning to their actions. They have not, like the humans, built up conflicting parallel structures to stumble over. One with nature, a bear is invincible, except in the matter of smell. I have heard it said that the only way to catch a bear in these mountains is to chase it downhill, to run after it so that the man follows its scent and not the other way around. It is then possible, I believe, to chain and enslave a bear, to make it bend to man's will: it will dance and snarl on order, and feed upon the leftovers of the humans, and if it still dreams of the cave where it once hibernated in the cold Himalayan winter and drew sustenance from the earth, why then it can still resort to dreaming and build up the cave again in its slow careful mind, and return to it even as its body indulges in ludicrous acts for the amusement of the other race.

The meditations of the frost, the abandon of the snow and now the presence of the bears, of these noble and ponderous creatures, gave me great joy. They brought ease and quiet and gentleness to this house. They led me back to where I belonged; I had strayed too far into the petty chaos of your world.

It was Father Benedictus who lured me, corrupted me with the temptations of words. Now I seek a voice. Every sound presupposes a listener. Every resonance seeks the reassurance of an echo. My words search the utterance of a voice.

I.iii

This is at bottom the only courage that is demanded of us: to have courage for the most strange, the most inexplicable.

Rainer Maria Rilke

Cannabis flourishes everywhere in our hills. The sacred hemp plant, the *bhang*, is only planted in the dark of a moonless Amavasya night to fully realise its potential as a window to other worlds and realities. I had *bhang* once by accident as a child: I had it on Holi in a fried bhaji that was not meant to find its way to me. My mind floated away and for hours I was delirious with the joy of discovery. Something similar is happening to me again, except that there is no joy in these deliriums. Who are these people and what are they doing to me?

Bhang is a way of life here: its seeds flavour the potatoes I eat, and the *bhang* chutney which Lohaniju makes so superbly is rivalled only by his lemon-radish-*bhang* relish. Cannabis is an innocuous-looking plant. It grows quietly on the hillsides, long-lived, limbed, supple, sympathetic, helpful. Significantly, it's only the female plant that is used to stimulate the mind. The male cannabis, which is taller and stronger, is used for hemp fibre, to make rope for the locals, or to weave a rough sackcloth. I was always slightly amused by the outrage our bhang causes in the big world outside; for us, it is a friend and confidante, a consolation and support rather than a hallucinogen.

The women in our hills don't take it as a drug – only as a medicine sometimes, or a poultice for a swollen leg or an infection. It's only the Mais, the Shaktins and Sanyasinis, the power women, part mendicant, part mystic, who roam these mountains dressed in black rags, a holy madness dripping from their eyes – it is only these women who take the drug. One such woman wandered into the house a few days ago. It had rained through the week. The ground was wet and the air was distinctly cold. She was wearing nothing at all, she was naked under the blue sky. I saw her from the upstairs window as she wandered into the garden – a tall gaunt figure, a skeleton almost, her dirty dishevelled hair covering her drooping breasts. There was really something compelling and powerful about her, a dignity in her nakedness and vulnerability. She had a vacant smile and very strong white teeth. She was smiling to herself, at the mountains, at the sky above. A butterfly, a pretty yellow butterfly, fluttered by and alighted upon her shoulder. Hesitating a moment, it settled upon her hair. It was a most incongruous sight, and then Lohaniju rushed out of the house and threw a blanket over her.

She didn't protest, but continued walking towards the house. She settled down on the steps leading from the veranda to the garden, and stared pensively in the direction of the snow mountains, which were no longer visible: a blanket of sudden fog and mist had obscured them. I felt tempted to go down and talk to her, but I knew it was not yet time. Some drama, some incident, had surely to enact itself in a visitation that began with such portent.

Lohaniju had disappeared into the house, and now he materialised again, a tray of food in his hands, some rice, some vegetables, some pickles. He placed the heavy brass *thali* before her, as well as a steel tumbler full of water. He tiptoed out, leaving her alone to stare at the mountaintops. Nothing happened, she just sat there all day, I could no longer spy her from the window. I tiptoed downstairs to check on her movements. She laid the blanket out like a rug and fell asleep on it, her head nestling in the crook of her arm, a naked woman exposed but not defenceless against the elements. Lady, our *bhotia* dog, was curled up at her feet. A swallow was feeding on the morsels of rice still remaining in her brass *thali*.

A kestrel streaked down against the clouded blue of the late afternoon sky, swooping low into the veranda, scaring away the feasting swallows. A long coil of speckled grey and black slipped from its beak and descended upon the sleeping Sanyasini. The snake fell with a thud upon the undernourished breasts and the jutting bones of her thin ribcage. Lady looked up cautiously, frozen into startled attention, but the sure, slow breathing from the sleeping body continued undisturbed. The serpent insinuated itself under her hair and around her neck, like a garland. Now she awoke. Rising to her full height she turned around to glimpse me cowering behind the mesh door from where I had been spying upon her. She opened the door and stared at me for a long time, her right hand gripping the brass door handle. With her left hand she patted me gently on both cheeks, on my scarred pitted cratered cheeks, and I swooned with terror as I encountered the viperous spite in the snake's glittering beady eyes, its fangs bared in the slightest suggestion of a snarl. It is really quite possible that I fainted at that point. I have no memory of what happened next, it was not so much fear or emotional exhaustion as the sheer intensity of the experience.

Lohaniju came up with my afternoon tea. He was strangely reluctant to discuss the naked woman. 'Has she ever come here before?' I asked him. 'Do you know her? Have you heard of her?'

Lohaniju stared ahead through me, towards the open window, where the evening mist swirled and obscured the sunset. His eyes were blank. 'I've never seen her before, Bitiya,' he said. His ears in their gold ear-hoops were twitching. He was lying, or at least evading the truth.

'Tell me, Lohaniju, please! You just have to tell me all that you know about her!' I insisted. I was frantic to know more about the visitation.

'I don't know her, but I have heard of her,' he said evasively. 'She is a follower of Baba Gorakhnath. Some people call her a madwoman. Some call her a sorceress. Women who are troubled by an excess of strength seek her out in the forest. She was married to the village Head-man, to the *Pradhan* many years ago. He used to ill-treat her, it is said. She had to get water for the household from many miles away. One day, as she was returning from the spring, she held the vessel of water against her thigh, rather than on her head, as her husband had instructed her to. Her husband saw her as she was returning to the village, and he kicked her vessel in anger. It fell to the ground and the water flowed out.

'It is said that something in this woman changed at that moment. Her eyes flashed fire and before he knew what was happening her husband stood transformed into a buffalo. A spring of fresh water flowed magically near his hooves. The villagers had seen all this happen. They knew then that she was a witch, not a woman. They stripped her naked and drove her out of the village. Even her children didn't protest.'

'This Mai is a scourge of male spirits, a healer and nourisher of the female spirit. I'm a man, I mustn't anger her at any cost. That's why I'm being so careful.'

I couldn't keep away. I crept down the stairs and stared at the empty veranda where the Mai had slept. I longed to talk to her, but it was too late. I recognised something of myself in her, some imbalance of strength, some distortion of gender. She had been spared the study of English Literature, and I, I had my clothes on.

One day my walk took me a longer way from home than usual. I trekked all the way up the hill, towards Chaubatiya. The glimmering line of Himalayan peaks to my left – Chaukhamba, Nanda Devi, Nanda Kot, Panchula was veiled in a gentle evening mist. I had covered my face with a black chiffon dupatta beneath which I felt cocooned, private, anonymous. I had on comfortable walking shoes; they led me where they wanted. I felt I was walking on air.

I found myself on the rocky path that leads to the Bhairav mandir, dedicated to the fiercest of our hill deities. The temple is a forbidding place. It is situated upon a curve of the hill which the sun never visits. A jagged assembly of boulders lines the way to the temple gates. A concatenation of crows are always squabbling there. Several steps up, on the spine of a ridge that straddles the mountainscape, in a direction obverse to the lay of the land, the Bhairav temple used to terrify me even as a child. Now, once again, the hair on my arms stood on edge as I walked up the sombre path. I could of course have turned back, but I am a stickler for courage in the face of obvious fear. Not for me the discretion which is the better part of valour. Life, head on, or not at all – that's the motto. Some day I shall surely be hoist by my own petard – the first traitor being this borrowed and plumaging language, this corrupter of thought. I shall abandon it, some day, and return to the tongue of my ancestors, to the dialect of my tribe.

I walked up towards the temple in silence, my face covered with the black dupatta, my shoes plodding upon their expensive air-pocketed soles. Even through the chiffon my nostrils were accosted by the acrid smell of smoke and burnt flesh, which floated up on the wings of the unseasonal fog-banks. Somewhere, not very far away, somebody was playing a plaintive Raag-Pahari upon a bamboo flute.

I hate the flute, it's a bit like poetry, it distorts emotion, cheapens it, rams it down your throat. It's simply too pretty to be real. It all appeared somehow staged – the stark landscape, the sad strains of the flute, all the props, all the cues, emotions to order. As usual, I put up a brave resistance, but the flute has an insidious way of getting under one's skin. It's cloying, it's creepy, it's crawly, it's crepuscular, but I couldn't really shut it out; I would be dishonest if I said I did.

I am very suggestible, and an immense sadness overtook me, a cosmic sadness, if I may use the word without sounding comical. Only the distant Himalayas continued to reassure me in spite of their pink-and-grey postcard prettiness. Now the flute gave way to the drum, melancholy to percussion. As the sun set, as the bravara goodbye to the mountains amalgamated with the darkness, my well-soled feet began responding to a primal heartbeat that echoed and reverberated in the earth and stone I was walking upon. One Two One Two One Two Three. One Two One Two Three.

The stones around me loomed large and black, the sky suddenly leaden with undisclosed threat. I wanted to turn back, but it was already very dark. I wasn't sure of the way. I could borrow a torch, or the priest at the temple could send somebody to escort me on the long walk back to the house. In the temple, the bells were tolling. They differed in range and pitch, but there was a continuity to their sound, a sort of rollback, which reached to the core of my body senses and left my heart pounding. The air was by now viscous with smoke and incense and the melodic ringing of the bells. As I reached the last step that led to the mountaintop I wondered anew at the folly of my extended walk. In our hills, animal sacrifices are usually conducted mid-morning to late afternoon, but as I unlaced my imported walking shoes before the temple entrance I could smell the sharp taste of recently shed blood. A slaughtered lamb lay upon the small stone platform before the circular Agni-kund, its severed head placed compliantly before its huddled-up frame.

I am not a vegetarian any more but I was brought up as one. The dismembered animal was, frankly, a nauseous sight. I wanted to turn back home, but the childhood injunctions against panthers, wandering witches, and *daayans* and *twalls*, the phosphorescent pillars of light that terrified all the locals, all stilled my resolve.

As if to reassure me a large and loving *Bhotiya* puppy about to achieve doghood settled himself at my feet. There was a crowd of people around, and somebody offered me a glass of hot oversweetened tea. The drumming was beginning to throb and pound in my temples, and I was feeling distinctly disoriented.

The priest's acolyte, his cotton dhoti stained with blood, was busy carving the haunches of the sacrificial animal into neat manageable squares of flesh, each of which was then wrapped tidily in a large *Belva* leaf, tied up with string, and plonked into a basket for distribution in the neighbouring villages.

Meanwhile the *Hurkiyas* with their whirling stringed drums, had sprung into action. A young woman before me, wearing a blue velvet *ghagra* style skirt and khaki-coloured man's cardigan was tapping her feet impatiently to the beat. She had brass anklets tied to her feet: they resonated in time to the music, their sound lost and forlorn against the frenetic drumming of the *Hurkiyas.* The crowd around me, which had settled down by now, was humming along with her in a low, exhausted monotone – a collective whisper, long slow monosyllables that made no sense in my vocabulary or syntax.

Weave a circle round him thrice,
And close your eyes with holy dread,
For he on honey-dew hath fed,
And drunk the milk of Paradise.

My life, as you can see, is a series of conditioned responses, and as usual I had found a suitable literary handle to hang on to, an echo that dismissed the need for primary and original reaction. A scavenger of the secondary sources, as it were.

Another woman was waving a censer before me, and a shower of dust and incense fell upon my black chiffon dupatta The other woman was dancing with more energy than ever before, her long skirt whirling around her, a dervish dance of trailing velvet, fat calves, bright eyes that seemed about to burst their sockets. A young man with a silly grin and a handkerchief tied around his forehead got up from the crowd and began dancing along with her. He held another handkerchief in his hands, which he was twirling around with an air of great importance.

I realised that I was witnessing a *jagar,* the ritual spiritual possession-exorcism dance where Ama and Bhairav are invoked, where old night reigns, where all the hunger for the unexpressed and the apocryphal finds utterance in a long and lingering blood-dance.

That sounds grander than it actually is: it's a sort of group yearning really, a local discotheque with the village idiot and his rendition of 'Light my Fire'. I'm not being facetious, really.

Well, the two of them went into a trance, and another man from the audience with glazed eyes and a fixed smile entered the fray, and then another until, tired of their village antics, I decided to walk home alone.

It was a Chaturdashi night, the full moon was just another day away. Everything around me was bathed in the sparkle and brilliance of a silvered understanding. My shadow wobbled before me, like a probe, and the night was full of rich sights and sharp smells that I was suddenly hungry to experience.

At a turn in the road I met a woman. I knew she was a witch from the way she looked at me. Her eyes bulged from their sockets, they were vacant and yet extraordinarily knowing. Her feet, of course, pointed backwards, at the past, at perversity, at pain. She bowed low before me, and her grotesque witch's face became for a moment calm, controlled, cloudlike.

Versed in the way of the world, I bowed back. She bowed again, and then, in a stagey, elocutionary manner, she recited a verse to me. I felt an immense pressure on my cranium, over my right lobe, and I suspected that I was hallucinating, for it was a poem I knew I had encountered before.

'Many paths lead from
the foot of the mountain
But at the peak

We all gaze at the
Single bright moon'

I bowed low before her, to acknowledge the beauty of the verse, even as the moonlight nudged at her face, my hands, my feet.

As if on cue, I was moved to reply.

'If at the end of our journey
There is no final
Resting place.
Then we need not fear
Losing our way.'

We smiled at each other. Our paths crossed. I hurried homewards, not afraid, indeed elated beyond belief. Above me, the cratered face of the white moon smiled benignly at the dark earth. Lohaniju was waiting for me by the bamboo thicket at the front gate. He had a torch in his hand. I wondered why he hadn't ventured any further to search for me. But then, he hated to leave the house.

In retrospect, the only thing that puzzles me, the missing fragment, is the language in which we communicated. Not English, not Hindi, not Pahari. The language of demotic moonlight, of lunatics and desperate fictionalisers. Perhaps.

The morning after my visit to the temple another strange woman came to visit me. She wasn't all that strange on the face of it, a plump, comforting, middle-aged woman with laugh lines that radiated from her eyes and her nose and converged in semicircles around her chafed red cheeks. She was the wife of the temple priest, he had sent her to me with some *prasada* – not the sacrificial lamb, thankfully, but a coconut, two pears, and a mangled mess of sweet *batashas, mithai* and marigold flowers. I had been recognised in the temple the night before, and the *prasada* was an acknowledgement of my visit.

As is the way with village woman, she started off with gossip and innuendo as soon as her immediate task of delivering the plastic bag containing the *prasada* was accomplished.

'You poor thing . . . you poor little thing!' she whispered commiseratingly, chucking me under the chin and stroking my shoulders. I recoiled from her touch; I felt raw and exposed. I was furious with Lohaniju for letting her in without my permission. Yet I had to be polite, for the gods are the gods and a temple is a temple: she was the wife of the priest, she had come to give me *prasada.*

Although I was fuming inside, my teeth were bared in a half-smile. As she continued with her inane talk I noticed an incongruous detail. Although we were sitting on the cane sofa set in the upstairs landing, which gets the morning sunlight, and although she was squinting from the bright morning glare, *yet she cast no shadow.* This detail terrified me inordinately, it was the final straw in the cumulative dementia that was slowly destroying me.

Lady had sensed something or someone. The fur on her back stood up in a familiar ridge, her speckled twist of tail bristled in alarm and aggression. I tried to distract her with a biscuit, but it didn't work; she was running in circles around the room, on some improbable invisible trail.

I turned back to catch my own shadow, and there it was, the good and faithful creature. My eyes wandered to her again, and there she was, outlined against the cane and flowered chintz, not even a suspicion of a shadow to cushion her corporeality.

Something was very wrong. 'Please don't go anywhere,' I told the priest's wife, 'please stay here until I call Lohaniju. He wants to talk to you, I know he does.' Then I ran all the way to the servants' quarters, where Lohaniju was sitting on the steps outside his room, contemplating an unlit cheroot. I didn't even have to speak to him, he could tell from my face that something was wrong. Wordlessly he followed me back to the house.

She was still sitting there when we returned, she had taken out her knitting in my absence, she was clicking away at her size ten needles, at a very long sleeve of multicoloured wool.

Lohaniju sat down on the floor, squatting on his haunches on the jute matting. He never presumes to sit on a chair inside the house, it's a point of honour with him. The priest's wife put her knitting aside, and began talking about Lohaniju's daughter, about his wife's sister's husband who had fallen from a walnut tree and fractured his leg, about the two-headed calf that had given birth in a neighbouring village. I stared at her intently. A nimbus of shade mimicked her movements, and a shadow fell behind her, quite as it should have.

She put a *pithya* my forehead before she left – a fingerful of damp vermilion with a few grains of rice, dot on the centre of my eyebrows. 'Phalo, phoolo, saubhagyavati bhava,' she murmured, and even as she gave me the benediction Lohaniju lifted his eyebrows and enacted an entire pantomime to indicate that I was respectfully to bow down and touch her feet, but I didn't. I had no desire whatsoever to flower, to fructify, to be blessed with matrimony – I rejected her benediction.

She picked up her knitting and, after a series of long goodbyes, readied herself for departure. I was still wary and watchful: she had violated my privacy; I couldn't trust my senses; I couldn't handle social encounters.

I wondered about the shadow – it had probably been some trick of the light. Living alone is driving me batty. It is time to rein in my imagination. I am in danger of getting lost in my internal labyrinths. It is time to regain a sense of perspective. But then, perspective is an illusion too – it's simply that some illusions are necessary markers for sanity, while others destroy that delicate balance. The convention of perspective seeks to represent a three-dimensional object upon a two-dimensional surface. As with these trick lines which approach a vanishing point to represent the third dimension of depth, so it is with words, with the verbal envoys of experience, the usurpers of reality.

I have no more books left to read, nothing with which to fight sleep and my suspect imagination. I read and re-read what I have been writing. The habit of over-articulation will surely strike me dumb one day. Blame it on the literary sensibility – blame it on what you please. Time to pull myself together, time to tread the straight and narrow.

Perhaps Anand hadn't wanted to die. Perhaps he had wanted to live. Even as he kicked the chair, balanced on a table, climbed towards eternity and the ceiling fan, even as the chair fell over with a crash, perhaps the core of him had cried that it still wanted to live.

Anand usually messed up whatever it was that he was doing. Tough shit that he had succeeded this one time. It wouldn't happen again, that's for sure!

Gallows humour is a phenomenon related to displaced anxiety and the denial of mortality. In a nutshell, I was alive and he was dead. That is the premise we must proceed upon.

*

Lohaniju was unwell yesterday. I had always thought of him as being somehow immortal, outside the framework of a lifespan. Never in my memory had he looked any younger or older than he did now. If one goes into chronology one has to conclude that he was about eighty years old, but his extreme agility belies such advanced years. His great height makes his long thin legs appear somehow awkward, for there is something incongruously adolescent about them.

Lohaniju had been coughing a lot recently, and sometimes he would stop to catch his breath while climbing upstairs. Yet I was so very self-absorbed that the very idea of Lohaniju's falling ill appeared quite outside the range of probable events. One morning I found him sitting by the fireplace, doubled over in pain. His forehead was beaded with sweat, and his eyes looked distant, they had a sort of fuzzy gleam around the pupils. He was panting, and I could sense the violent flutter of his heart against his ribcage. Something had happened to his hair – it seemed to glow with a strange blue light, as though he had had a blue rinse at the hairdresser's. His hair had spread out like a halo, it had assumed a life of its own and stood up like an unruly mob in a stadium when a match is over. He was feverish to the touch, and he seemed to be looking over my shoulder at something that wasn't there.

'My time has come,' he said. 'I'm afraid, Bitiya, that my time has come at last.'

Just then, the ancient clock that hung on the panelled wall by the landing, next to the lacquer screen that I had always coveted (the lacquer screen I always planned to take back to Delhi), this ancient clock, which had been mute ever since I could remember, suddenly groaned and clanked and made sounds of rigorous toil and exercise, then struck up a clamour of uncoordinated chimes.

I was so startled that I almost jumped out of my skin. Lohaniju too seemed a bit surprised. His eyes rolled about their orbits in an absolutely unnerving way, and he put his hands to his ears to shut out the din.

The scene reeked of melodrama and high histrionics. It was like a term paper upon 'Some Conventions of the Gothic'. The chain of causality between lightning (preferably forked), black cats and cruel hysterical laughter, as also rusty clocks and antique furniture, the signature of the genre, was at work. I resented being roped into such a predictable script, and resolved to make my escape.

The clock had resumed a steady, energetic chime. It had certainly succeeded in shaking Lohaniju out of his pallor – he leapt up and started climbing upstairs again. 'Only three o'clock,' he said, in his best story voice. 'There's life in the old soldier yet!'

I wondered whether he was referring to the clock or to himself. 'I found the key in the kitchen godown yesterday,' he said, his gold hoops glinting in the warm rays of the afternoon sun. 'I wound up the clock last afternoon. Why it chose to come to life this afternoon is a mystery I cannot explain. It's a made in England clock, it belonged to an English missionary and his wife. He was too sure about his God, that padre, of his made in England God. The clock is still working, and I'm sure his God is too, but the Lords who rule our landscape have to be placated in their own ways.'

So much for the anomalies of time. 'You couldn't have been born when the house was built,' I protested; 'you're not so old, Lohaniju!'

'Time moves in circles, Bitiya,' he said reprovingly. 'Of course I remember the Padre, and all the others who have lived here. After all, I'm the guardian of the house, aren't I?'

I decided to humour him. He was an old man and he hadn't been keeping well. 'Of course you are, Lohaniju,' I said. 'After all, you belong to his house, don't you?'

'I belong to this house, and this house belongs to me,' he said dreamily. Again his eyes held the distant look which had alarmed me earlier in the afternoon. 'All the sahibs and memsahibs who lived here on this hill where our Lord Airee lives . . . It's his secrets we protect, his strength that we live by. The spine of the mountain is a sacred spot, a forbidden spot. There are places in our mountains which are like that – they have guardian spirits that don't like people. These spots are conjunctions between the worlds. It's not that they are good spots or bad spots – they are simply passages, points of entry and exit.

'The missionary was foolish to build his house in this lonely spot. We hill people prefer to live together, near each other; humans need each other, it's pride to think that they don't. Besides, he knew that this was a sacred spot, and that the arrows of Lord Airee lie buried here, deep in the soil, below the rock, even. These arrows never rust, and when the time comes the Gods will deign to use them once again. The guardians of our hills have to be protected, kept secret even from the brahmins and the common folk. What do the common folk know, after all?'

He was talking much too much, and I was worried for his health. The clock began its hideous groaning and clanging, like a guillotine being oiled, and struck the half-hour.

'What do the common folk understand? That the sun rises and sets, that crops prosper or fail, that humans live and then die? The common folk know nothing, Bitiya! Believe me, they understand nothing! The sun neither rises nor sets, it is our earth that moves. Prosper or fail, it is all the same in the end – if there is an end, that is. People neither live nor die, they just move houses, and bodies, and dimensions. What is it that the priests know? How to appease the Gods, how to offer sacrifice, how to beg before the people, how to beg of the Gods! Our Lord Airee, he is a strange one, he is! He does not need to have garlands and marigolds, incense and coconuts offered to him! He despises the homage of the ignorant. He seeks strength and courage and a fearless disposition, and the only worship you can do him is to send the arrow of your actions straight from the strung bow of your resolution.'

It was the longest speech I had ever heard him make. His face was a grey and ashen colour, his voice shook, he looked as though he might dematerialise and disintegrate right there before me.

I made him sit down on the sofa on the upstairs landing. He was always stubborn about sitting down before the *sahib-log*, but today he was too tired to protest. He was agitated and nervous, he was breathing in gulps and gasps. I held his hands to comfort him, his leathery, scaly, workworn hands. They gave back more strength than I gave to them.

After a while his breathing returned to normal. 'I'll go back to my room now, Bitiya,' he said. 'I've talked too much for one day – or for a lifetime, even.' I tried to help him up but he signalled me away. 'There's life in the old soldier yet,' he repeated, and got to his feet again without any visible strain. Resisting my offers of help, he started off for his room. I followed him up to the front door, but he wouldn't let me come any further. 'My daughter will be coming to visit me today,' he said. 'A glass of warm milk and I'll be back to shape again. There's life in the old soldier yet!'

On the landing, the clock had resumed its contorted cacophony of sound. I shook it violently, until I thought it would fall off the wall, but this only accelerated the movement of the pendulum, and it began hyperventilating at estimably a hundred and twenty seconds to the minute. Frantic, I wedged open the glass front and held on to the pendulum until it came to a complete halt. Then I yanked it off the body of the clock, leaning it against the musty wood cabinet, and shut the glass front firmly back in place.

Sometimes, silence is the greatest blessing in all the world. I sat down in my room and savoured the sounds of sunlight and breeze. I could hear the rustle of pine-needles, and I could feel the shadowed presence of a tree outside the window. The tree presence filled the room with pine scent and cypress sighs. Something gentle, something redeeming and forgiving, overflowed from the window into the room. It relaxed the tight muscles of my back, it loosened the iron crunch of the rubber band that held my hair tied back in a punitive loop. It massaged my cratered skin, my ravished eyebrows, my dry lips, until they forgot their conditioning of stealth and despair. It made me want to smile.

My sister telephoned again last week. She has come up with another of her optimistic long-distance solutions. 'Why don't you write a novel?' she said, as though she was suggesting that I bake a cake, or get my hair permed. 'You know, sort of bleed the pain and let it all hang out.' I told her that I was in no pain, I was merely in retreat, but the thought had found a harbour in my expectations.

I toyed with the idea for a while before rejecting it. I will resist the urge to articulate, to simplify, to gloss over, to impose patterns that are nothing but a comforting construct. I will not become another fictionaliser. There are some emotions that words can only betray. Better to be careful. Better to be silent. I will outwit the game. I will not become; sometimes it is enough to be.

I am dithering. All night long I listen to the Doors, the same tracks again and again. Never to Kishore Kumar. Lohaniju has begun to keep to himself, he has been running a temperature for a week. His daughter is living with him, she prepares my meals, she is not as good a cook as he is. I am getting near the end of my resources. It is as though my field of vision is narrowing. I know already that these are classic symptom of hysteria, but I've discovered that knowing things is no help at all. Out of the corners of my eye I can see two parallel walls of darkness creeping up behind me on either side. I know that when these two walls of darkness meet, I shall be broken. Fiction is the last recourse of one threatened by certainty. Or is it the other way around?

Today I distinctly heard an inner voice speak. It whispered from the debris of clamorous emptiness that is my centre. It said to me, 'Hang on. Just hang on. OK?'

Last night I slept the sleep of the innocent. The fluctuating electricity, the wavering shadows, these things didn't bother me at all. All through the night I listened to the dull splatter of rain on the slate roof. It reached through my dreaming to some recess of my mind where its constant percussion lulled me into further security. I dreamt that I was having a dream from which I dreamt that I woke up. Sleep and dream and awakening merged into a circular connectedness. When I awoke, that is to say, when dawn broke and the certainties of the morning like birds chirping and the first ray of sunlight illumining the Nanda Devi peak through the distant mist and fog – when dawn broke I felt all right. I felt as though I had the right to exist, as though I was a part of creation, of the dawn chorus, of the healing sunlight that was showing up in shy dappled patches in the garden. I was a glob of consciousness, of reactions and conditioning, enveloped in skin (damaged skin, but nevertheless). I was defined in time and space and dimension. I had the right to exist!

That was the breakthrough, the sudden insight into my innocence, my lack of culpability, my exoneration.

Proprioception is the science of the sense of self. My centre, my identity, my selfhood had for a while abandoned the confines of skin and bone, abandoned my cage and run away to cower in dusty corners of other abandoned memories and perceptions. Dona Rosa and the rest are not real, they do not belong any longer to this clear and unquestioning morning, they are emanations of the past, insubstantial, evasive, ambiguous. I am alive, a skin-encapsulated being who belongs inalienably to the world of the living. I feel as though a scab has fallen from an old sore. In the shadow world between the living and the unliving, even sickness is an indication of possible restoration to health.

In the long-ago days when I still taught in college, when I was a popular teacher and a desirable young woman engaged to an aspiring genius, I had taught a paper on the novel. The novel introduces order into disorder, it culls selectively from random and diverse sources, it conspires with the author's consciousness to play dice or God with the universe, as the fashion may be. The novel is a lying, deceitful mechanism, it leads its readers into an unnatural addiction to order and resolution and other such compulsive fictionalising.

I remembered that long-ago classroom in Delhi, the nuns in their bleached white habits sternly patrolling the disinfected corridors. Thirty young girls stared and stared at their textbooks, while their lives stretched before them like numinous shadows. Thirty young girls awaited my instruction.

We were doing *Aspects of the Novel.* 'Only connect,' I told them, 'only connect.' Forster was right, I suppose, but life, unlike the novel, is about disconnectedness. The desire to render comprehensible, to reduce and to simplify, is a disease of the human race. When I was in hospital my sister had brought me a jigsaw puzzle as a present, in a large cardboard box with a picture of a garden on it. It was a garden in unnatural bloom, it had a violent sense of energy which made me feel even more ill. I struggled with the pieces for days, but the lupins and larkspurs would collide into each other's spaces, and I couldn't tell the mud from the gravel path, or the sky from the reflecting lake below. I put all my energy into the puzzle. The Malayah nurse had stared at me with incomprehension and vague scorn, yet her touch when she sponged my body was gentle.

Sometimes, in life (unlike in fiction) the search for order falsifies. Dissociation is as important as association. Forster stood discredited, at least for a while. The key phrase was different. 'Only disconnect.'

I had been trapped in a confusion of second-hand perceptions, confounded by the treachery of words. My language-clogged consciousness had led me astray. We do not see things as they are, we see them as we are. The lover creates the loved one by projection. Narcissistic love is an act of incest. Of course I had never loved Anand.

The redemption of language is a long and infinitely arduous task. Silence is the precondition of speech. The texture of life has to be experienced, not spoken about. Without the polarity of silence, language would not exist. All this and more I knew suddenly that morning when I awoke from a night of rain-drummed dreams. All of us have experienced moments when the ordinary becomes extraordinary, when mind and body are graced by some redeeming joy that is both of this world and not of it. Some passing angel had graced me with the gift of forgetting, purged me of the prophecy of pain.

I got another call from my sister. Our uncle in Bangalore, our mother's brother, the one who owns this house, had telephoned her, which was an event in itself. He is a hermetic man, a recluse, he could even be called eccentric. Our uncle had received an offer of sale for the house, an offer so fantastic and astronomical that it left me dumbstruck. My uncle, who had so far maintained a hands-off attitude to the sensational mess I had got myself into, seemed actually quite clued up as to what was happening. They had made enquiries, my sister said, a telltale squeak in her voice indicating excitement, and they had located a world-famous plastic surgeon of Indian descent from Austin, Texas who was coming to Delhi for a six-month break. 'He's a world-famous surgeon,' she said (she has a tendency to repeat herself), 'and he plans to take on a few select cases. He'll remake you – he said it would be an interesting exercise in reconstruction. He can lengthen your fingers – he can even give you dimples if you want. He's told me to put together a portfolio of your old photographs – the way you used to look. You should change the bridge of your nose, it was much too long the way it was! Rachita, Rachita, are you even listening to me!?'

The fault, dear Brutus is not in our stars but in ourselves. Dear God, will I ever leave Eng. Lit. behind me?

Meanwhile my sister was holding long distance from New Delhi. 'I'll think about it,' I said. The fleecy cloud of hope resettled into a familiar dark hatred. Of course it was a silly idea. I held on to the telephone for a long time after she had disconnected.

If you lose – if one loses one's sense of self, there is no remedy but to proceed on a simulated model. All self-image is anyway a construct of circumstance. If you lose an arm or a leg, you cannot forget what you have lost, the phantom pain is there to remind you, but if you have lost your sense of selfhood things are quite different, for (this is the important part) you are no longer there to know it. Who will find you again?

I felt like asking somebody – anybody – if I was really me at all. I needed an impartial examination into the whole thing.

For each of us in the human condition, there is a time, a moment, when all the contradictions, the circumlocutions, the discrepancies, the discordances, the jangling unease of being alive becomes as easy and magical as a juggler in control of his balls.

Some time after my sister telephoned me from Bangalore, after the echo of the crackle of the telephone, the buzz of her happy excited busy voice, had settled into the accustomed sombre silence that habituated the house, not even a drizzle to break the sound barrier, only the distant cry of mountain birds, the cawing of crows outside – only then did I have my stark second of absolute and unconditional truth.

It happened something like this: I was searching for a comb. My scalp felt dry, my hair was particularly limp, I hadn't washed it for days. A bad hair day is not just a modern consumerist construct: a bad hair day signifies a general lack of receptivity to the forces of the universe. Everything about me felt wrong, even my insides were a bit wonky, all those baked beans were beginning to have their foretold effect.

I was searching for a comb, it's better than a hairbrush sometimes, and I went to the dressing room, which is one step down from my bedroom, the dark damp dressing room with a musty smell and the huge misted-over mirror on the dresser. Well, I found the comb, and as I worked it through my tangled, tousled-up hair, from force of old habit I looked at the mirror.

I looked at the mirror . . . You have no concept of the scope and import of these words. I looked at the mirror, and, for the first time in months, I saw my face. You will make allowances for the fact that it was dark in the dressing room, that the mirror itself was only notionally a reflector of true images, but the point of the encounter was that I looked just fine – quite nice, really. I am thinner than I used to be, so the structure of my face showed better, and my shoulder-length hair left loose covered up a great deal of the damage that the pipette of hydrochloric acid had perpetuated. A little foundation, a slash of lipstick, and I could surely face the world again.

This sounds too simple to qualify for a genuine certifiable epiphany, but something about the dressing room, some trick of the light, led me to see not just my reflection but myself, the self I truly am. I love long words, I am addicted to them, it's a professional hazard, so you will excuse me if I express it this way: the deep disturbances in my self-image, my body ego, the sense of depersonalisation that was dogging me, simply vanished. I looked in the mirror and saw myself. It was as easy as that.

Eye dew embarrasses me. I never cry. My eyes smart only when I am angry or extremely irritated. But here it was, I was actually weeping, my lashes were heaving with the successive weight of about-to-be-shed tears. I looked in the mirror again, through a blur of tears, and thankfully, I was still there.

*

This is the most beautiful time of the year in our hills. The leaves begin to change colour, and a shadow of red sits upon the hillside. The marigolds are out in full bloom, their rich smells satiate the senses. The tribulations of winter are just around the corner, yet the last snatches of sun-drenched joy still saturate the earth. Marrows sit plumply upon the sloping roofs of village houses, sunning themselves, and tomatoes are dried and preserved for the sunless winter. Corn hangs by the eaves of Lohaniju's cottage, as do garlands of bright red chillies. The Himalayas gleam brightly in the warm clear sunlight, and when the first snows fall in the high reaches of the mountains, powdering the peaks with an added glow, there is something breathtaking and stupendous in their beauty. It is a time to harvest, to conserve, to await a trial of strength with the elements. It is a time of joy and resolution.

Well, there's no denying it. I had succumbed to the pressure, to the guilt. My body was the culprit, my wanton body that loved warmth and celebration, my body which had done what it should not have, my body which has paid the price. My mind has stood by me, my stubborn denying mind, but it has abandoned my body, leaving it vulnerable to anger, abuse and invasion. My mind has now to negotiate a truce with that body, return from its exile and wanderings to the homestead of my limbs, the hearth of my hungers. It is so very simple.

It is not my body that has betrayed me – it is I who have betrayed this body. My abandonment of courage has been no less treacherous than Anand's. Courage is not simply a virtue – it is the testing point of all virtues at the highest conflux of reality. I will not fail this test of courage – I will venture unafraid into the future, with my body, with my mind, with my spirit. Everything is so simple, really.

I tried to explain some of this to my sister on the telephone. She suggested that I talk to a psychotherapist. 'I think you are going round the bend,' she said. 'I think you need professional help. I hope you've been thinking seriously about the cosmetic surgery.' She gave me the number of a doctor who ran a helpline. I booked a call. It was a wrong number. She called back again, with the right number this time. 'I've talked to Dr Bhatia,' she said, talking louder than was necessary, 'and he is waiting for your call. He is waiting for your call, Rachita.'

The long-distance lines were down, but I got across somehow. Dr Bhatia had a flat, opaque voice, a voice without contours or intonation. I tried to visualise him, what he must look like. Bald, perhaps, and he must surely be wearing spectacles. He seemed completely uninterested in what I had to say.

'Doctor, I'm seeing things,' I said, 'things that aren't there, I mean. I'm imagining things. I'm hallucinating. There's something wrong with me.'

There was a moment's silence, and a polite prefatory cough. 'I believe you live alone, Miss Rachita,' he said, a little hesitantly. 'Well, in conditions of sensory isolation, the human input channels tend to become filled with discordant signals. In common language, people begin to hallucinate.'

'Thank you, Doctor,' I murmured, and put the phone down. Dona Rosa had just sauntered into the room. She settled herself before the fireplace. I could see the flames, I could hear the hiss and spit of the fire. Who had felled this stump of oak, who had brought in these pine-cones and lit the fire? Where was the *sagar* we always used?

There was the sound of banging on the front door. I went downstairs to open it.

I had a visitor. It was Zenobia Desai, my least favourite student, the bane of my academic life. I found her fat and profound face bathed in the dying sunset staring at me with what was undeniably concern and even love. 'Rachita, Ma'am,' she exclaimed, 'it's so good to see you again! I wanted to meet you so I got your address from the college!'

I have become so trained in revulsion towards my species that I banged the door shut upon her face. As I was walking up the staircase the callousness of my action struck me, and caused me enough remorse for me to retrace my steps and go back to find her. She was still standing by the door. Her face dissolved in relief when she saw me. Of course I had no option but to let her in, and she oohed and aahed at the beauty of the old house, decrepit as it was.

One thing is certain – I cannot teach again. Never ever can I summon the certitude to face a classful of critical adolescents. In my room upstairs I found Dona Rosa brushing her hair, and wondered whether to introduce her to Zenobia. I thought better of it, and went in search of Lohaniju's daughter to get her to make us some tea.

Lohaniju was in a bad way, he was coughing and wheezing dreadfully and his face was a dull ashen colour. I observed that I was taking charge, the way I did in those long-ago days when I was still real. I brought a thermometer from the house, and checked Lohaniju's temperature. It was higher than I had suspected. I telephoned the doctor, and he promised to send for a taxi and make a house call. 'Please admit him to the military hospital if need be,' I heard myself say. 'I'll talk to the Colonel of the regiment if there is any difficulty about admitting him.' Yes, there was no mistake about it, it was my old voice again, my authoritative teacher's voice.

I didn't flinch when the doctor came in, and I was neither embarrassed nor angry when he averted his eyes after one hurried look at my face. I led him to Lohaniju's room, Zenobia trailing behind us wielding her torch like a light-sword. Lohaniju was bundled into the taxi and taken to the military hospital. His daughter accompanied him, and Zenobia and I returned to the house.

Dona Rosa was trying to attract my attention. 'You are getting distracted,' she said animatedly, her red lips glinting against her sparkling teeth. 'You're forgetting where you really belong. Come back here while there's still time.'

A glass of milk, which Lohaniju's daughter had left on the wooden mantelpiece above the fireplace, suddenly levitated a few inches from the surface of the wood, as though lifted by an invisible hand. It hovered uncertainly for a moment, and then, overcome by the forces of gravity, came crashing down to the floor, where the glass lay shattered as a river of milk flowed like an oblation into the disused fireplace.

Lady walked into the room. I had not realised that she was carrying. She was panting, her trusting dog-eyes were puzzled by the pain she was encountering. She lay down on the rug by my bed. Soft squeals escaped her at increasingly regular intervals, then suddenly a small form slithered out of her. It was covered with wet and slime and blood. It was alive.

Zenobia was standing in the middle of the room, grave and still. For some reason her spectacles were frosted over, and her fat face had a faraway look. 'There are too many people in this room,' she said, in the earnest voice I knew so well. 'There are just too many people here. I have been here before, a long time ago, in this very house. But none of it matters any more. Please understand, Ma'am, please understand' (and here she shook me urgently by the shoulders, so close that I could smell her body odour and the giddy floral perfume that attempted to hide it), 'just understand, Ma'am, the past belongs only to the past.'

And indeed I could see Marcus and Munro, they were in a corner of the room, they were struggling to break through an invisible barrier. There was a loud banging at the front door: I couldn't for the life of me think who it might be. As I went down the staircase I could smell the strong sweet scent of incense, I could hear the sound of invisible footsteps scurrying silently up the staircase, bare feet on wood. As I opened the door there was an explosion of fireworks from the direction of Ranikhet town, and the smell of cordite in the air. Green and blue rockets left fluorescent flashes in the sky, and I realised that it was the night of Diwali, of the festival of light. Lohaniju's daughter had even managed to light a few earthen lamps by the veranda before she left; they were flickering bravely in the November breeze.

A white dove, white with hints of blue-green sheen on its plumage, flew into the veranda. A length of twine was tied to its feet, and this string got tangled up in the wooden balustrade that bordered the house. The dove fluttered about, it was agitated, it was in the wrong place at the wrong time, and then miraculously it broke loose of the mess of its bondage and flew away calmly into the unquiet night.

What fortitude the Soul Contains
That it can so endure

The accent of a coming Foot—
The opening of a Door

Ms Dickinson will you please vacate my fucking mind? And take your poetry with you!

A curly-haired young man stood at the door. He was incredibly tall – I had to crane my neck to look up at him. His face was spattered with acne. In spite of his frown, and the expression of grim concentration with which he greeted me, there was something reassuring about him.

'I'm Pashu,' he said, introducing himself. 'I'm Zenobia's boyfriend.'

'Is that short for Pashupati?' I felt compelled to ask.

'No, just Pashu,' he replied. 'May I come in?'

He was awkward when he walked, and I realised that he had a club foot. He was wearing a long heavy fur overcoat which he took off as he entered the hallway. His shoulder-length hair was lank and greasy. His sweatshirt had something printed on it. Reality Bytes, it said. He unbuttoned his overcoat, and turned around to hang it on the stand. Just his height reassured me, he was so very tall. Outside, the sky was still exploding with fire crackers, and the smell of gunpowder hung heavy on the stairs. My sari caught on a nail, and I stumbled and fell. He turned back and helped me up. He smelt of pine-leaves and mint and fresh apples.

Suddenly, my pulse quickened, and I felt the old familiar heightening of perception, the sense of doubled consciousness. Surrounded by a blur of motion, I saw the panthers, hungry, angry, green slits for eyes, the smell of flesh and fur, poetry in motion as they bounded up the stairs. They leapt right through me as though I didn't exist, and it was only because of Pashu's hand in mine, the safety of his touch, that I didn't faint from terror.

Upstairs, everything was quite normal. Lady had left her pup on the rug and wandered off somewhere. Zenobia had mopped up the mess of blood and placenta with an old sweater of mine which I was actually quite attached to. A howl of pain alerted me to Lady's presence on my counterpane. She had delivered another pup on my bed, she was viewing it with grave and steadfast eyes and licking its brown matted fur. And then the mystery of birth and life affirmed itself all over again, and a third squiggly creature tumbled out of her haunches right there before me. I was deeply moved. Lady turned to me trustfully; there was a look of triumph in her eyes as the newborn lives turned to her heavy teats for sustenance. How could I possibly not have registered that she was carrying?

Zenobia acknowledged Pashu's presence only casually. She was standing in the centre the room in an attitude of utmost concentration. The panthers were in the room too, but perhaps only I could see them for Zenobia and her boyfriend didn't react in the least to their growls. Dona Rosa had changed into a dress of electric blue silk, she had done up her hair in a most becoming way, and here she was eyeing Zenobia's friend with the utmost appreciation. Meanwhile, Marcus and Munro had disappeared, and there were no traces of fear or anger or any such emotions they might have left behind. Their hold was loosening.

There was a sudden chill breeze from behind me, from the window that faced the snow ranges. The curtain was stirring in the wind, stirring out to reach for Dona Rosa.

Pashu lit up a joint and the gentle smell of cannabis permeated the air. I was still wondering about his name, for Pashu is after all an odd name, when I heard a scream: it was Marcus, I was sure it was. Zenobia was still rooted in the centre of the room, she looked silly and inappropriate and posturing. Her moustache stood out prominently, beaded with sweat, but her eyes were luminescent with kindness and bathed in pain. A shining light suffused us all, a blue light with green edges. The thought floated through my mind that if Zenobia could find herself a boyfriend, surely I could, too. Nothing was impossible.

'What am I doing here at all?' Pashu said, the smoke from his cigarette suspended in clouds above his cratered face. 'I mean here in the world, not here in this house. You know, Rachita –' (Zenobia always called me Ma'am and here he had moved to my first name already!) '– I wasn't actually meant to be born at all. It's a dreadful misunderstanding, a mix-up. Even in my mother's womb, I sensed already that there had been a major fuck-up. I could hear her shouting at the servants, or gossiping while she played rummy at the Delhi Gymkhana Club, and I knew I was trapped in this erroneous fate. And now I just have to lump it in this lifetime, but it's terrible, it's like being lost in a fog, a grey struggle – like groping in the dark for a shadow. Zenobia is the only person with whom I can connect, who I knew from before.'

I listened with a degree of impatience. I really had very little time for other people's problems or preoccupations, but he continued regardless.

'It's only Zenobia who understands, I feel safe with Zenobia.'

I found that I was viewing Zenobia with deep and uncharacteristic affection, even veneration. She looked different somehow – she had a flowing white beard! No, that was plainly impossible! I was hallucinating! It had begun with the glass of milk. It had to be all those pills they had prescribed. I would throw them all away.

Now Zenobia was surrounded by a swarm of yellow butterflies. For some reason I wanted to kiss the hem of her skirt. And then there was another blur, and I felt lost and lonely, as though I was in withdrawal, not that I've been in withdrawal before. I wondered wildly if listening to the news broadcast on the BBC might somehow restore my sanity. The music system had a radio as well. I asked Pashu if he could help me tune in to the news. He looked puzzled, and ignored my request.

Pashu was reefing through the music. He had not even switched on the system when the most beautiful sounds, one could even call them celestial, cascaded through the room in waves and curtains of joy. The cosmic battle is conducted in the most phantasmagorical of daily playing fields. It is fought out in ordinary everyday ways which are not even perceived or picked up by the participants. Of this I am sure.

That cool sparkling pool of strength that had been my refuge when I was a child appeared before me. It was surrounded by ferns and flowers, and a sea of yellow butterflies danced in the sky above. Tremulous but unafraid, I stepped out of the armour of caution I had worn so many years and proceeded once again to that familiar place, to the landscape of certainty and sure action. It was not an illusion.

Lohaniju walked into the room. He looked younger than he had appeared for a long time, there was something different about his gait, it seemed smoother, as though he was floating on air. His gold earrings shone in the dim light, and he was tugging at his earlobes, a gentle smile on his dear beloved face.

I noticed that Anand was in the room as well, my once-beloved Anand who had committed suicide and effectively destroyed my life. Considering that it was Anand he was looking quite sorted out. He gave me a friendly smile that still reached to my heart, somehow. 'No hard feelings, baby,' he said: it sounded utterly incongruous from what was after all a ghost. A nervous giggle escaped me, the situation had quite lost its gravitas, this was not how Hamlet's father conducted himself.

'There are more things in this world, Rachita, than are dreamt of in your philosophy,' Anand declaimed, as though on cue. I decided that I was suffering from progressive dementia, and resolved to telephone my sister if only I could remember her number. I wanted desperately to be sane, to know and understand and belong to only one reality, one mode of belief.

'*Oh that I had never been to Wittenberg, never read a book!*'

Somewhere in another world I heard the telephone ring. There was a call from the hospital. Lohaniju was dead, he had died in the taxi on his way there. His daughter was taking his body home to her village, she had sent for her husband and father-in-law. I didn't need to come there at all. I felt no pain or surprise at the news.

To tread the step of faith, the step in the dark which is not there. Only Dona Rosa remained in the room: she was looking ravishingly beautiful, she was draped in a succession of shimmering veils. '*For one kiss wilt thou be willing to give all,*' she said, in a voice so low and so clear that it made my hair stand up on edge. There were goose pimples on my skin, and my nails were clenched so tight that they tore into the soft flesh of my palms and drew blood.

Dona Rosa handed something to me. The cool touch of her hand sent a shiver up my spine. She had given me a rose, a golden rose, with a long glittering stem, with thorns, with leaves, with petals. A perfectly formed rose of pure glistening gold.

'*For one kiss wilt thou be willing to give all,*' she said again, '*but whosoever gives one particle of dust shall lose all in that hour.*' She winked at me, a delicious, feminine, mischievous wink, and then she was gone.

The rose sat in my hands like a portent of joy. It was heavy, real, of this dimension. I could feel the delicate workmanship of the thorns. I looked at it in wonder.

To be ourselves we must remain in control of our scripts. We must make and remake ourselves, possess and repossess our world, cast and recast our lot, in every precious moment. Above all, we must know what to hold on to, what to discard, in this radical flux which is life.

I felt disquietingly alive. My repertoire of memory had run out: I had bid farewell to the world of my confabulations. I had acquired – achieved – possessed – myself again.

Zenobia and her boyfriend were caught in a passionate clinch, they were kissing each other as if there was no tomorrow. Or no yesterday. A firefly was fluttering around Zenobia's straight black hair, it surrounded her in a field of electric energy: in that dim light they were like young gods, the two of them, impregnable and pure of heart. I slunk out of the room, I had been incarcerated there too long, and made for the balcony, where the Milky Way glimmered like a string of candy floss in the incandescent sky. It was a moonless night, and an infinity of stars met my eyes. The most sensitive part of the retina is not at the centre of the field of view. You can best see far stars and other objects by averting your vision slightly.

As I looked up at the sky, the encroaching band of darkness that had threatened the periphery of my vision for so long suddenly disappeared. I had an ecstasy of understanding so sweet that it could not possibly be true. I knew then that I had travelled to the edge of my world, and returned, and that the world was good. The stars above bathed me in their love, and an ebullient sure strength surged through my blood, pounding and panting with the excitement of rebirth. Far away, the last of the Diwali lamps flickered in Ranikhet town.

My world had been undermined, taken apart, reduced to anarchy and chaos. And now, mysteriously, inexplicably, beatifically, it had reintegrated into something more than the sum of its parts. The most crucial matters continue to remain hidden because of their very ordinariness. We are unable to see the important things because they are right before our eyes. Wittgenstein said, 'The real foundations of his enquiry do not strike a man at all.' I think that's truer than we know.

Pain is a habit, pain is an orientation. It can be repudiated. It can be left behind. This house that had taken me in, where I had let loose my fears, hidden my shame – this house which had nurtured and healed me – was it now at last time to bid farewell to this house?

My foot was still hurting from my fall on the stairs. I hobbled back to the room. Zenobia and her boyfriend were asleep on the bed, next to Lady and her new litter. They had thrown the counterpane away, they were nestled in each other's arms like two spoons. Lady was sleeping too. She was breathing tiredly, her pups were asleep beside her. They were whimpering, their eyes were closed and they were suckling noisily at her teats even in their sleep, in the way puppies do. We breathed as though with one breath, we dreamed as though in one dream. It was a communion of the living. There was no one else in the room. A slight breeze stirred the curtains by the open window, while outside the unblinking snows stared sightlessly at the skies above.